From

hunted by death...

LEW SANDERS: He had served in OSS in World War II—fighting with Vietnam's Communists against the Japanese. Twenty years later he was back—on a mission to kill a friend.

JAI LAZAR: His grandfather was a Frenchman who once sang nursery rhymes to him. Now, his life had been transformed by violence, and he was on a desperate mission for Hanoi.

DAVE MCWATERS: A child of privilege and promise, the young Navy lieutenant was assigned to follow Sanders in Vietnam. What he would find was the wild horror of war—and the cruelty of betrayal.

AMBASSADOR ROBERT VOSSENACK: Sanders had served—and almost died—under him in Korea. In Vietnam they were part of the same mission, but they were enemies just the same...

ANNA VO: The beautiful Vietnamese movie actress appeared in kung fu films in Japan. McWaters fell head over heels for her—without knowing who she really was.

SHADOW TIGER

ATTENTION SCHOOLS AND CORPORATIONS

WARNER books are available at quantity discounts with bulk purchase for educational business or sales promotional use For information please write to SPECIAL SALES DEPARTMENT WARNER BOOKS 666 FIFTH AVENUE NEW YORK N Y 10103

ARE THERE WARNER BOOKS
YOU WANT BUT CANNOT FIND IN YOUR LOCAL STORES?

You can get any WARNER BOOKS title in print Simply send title and retail price plus 50¢ per order and 50¢ per copy to cover mailing and handling costs for each book desired New York State and California residents add applicable sales tax Enclose check or money order only, no cash please to WARNER BOOKS. P O BOX 690. NEW YORK, N Y 10019

SHADOW TIGER

BARRY TAYLOR

WARNER BOOKS

A Warner Communications Company

All the characters portrayed in this story are fictitious.

Page 82 excerpted from THE COLLECTED POEMS OF A.E. HOUSMAN, copyright 1922 by Holt, Rinehart, and Winston, Inc., and renewed 1950 by Barclays Bank Ltd. Reprinted by permission of Henry Holt and Company, Inc.

WARNER BOOKS EDITION

Copyright © 1989 by Barry Taylor
All rights reserved. No part of this book may be reproduced or transmitted in any form or by any means, electronic or mechanical, including photocopying, recording, or by any information storage and retrieval system, without permission in writing from the Publisher.

This Warner Books Edition is published by arrangement with the Walker Publishing Company, Inc.

Cover design by Joe Curcio
Cover illustration by Joe Devito

Warner Books, Inc.
666 Fifth Avenue
New York, N.Y. 10103

A Warner Communications Company

Printed in the United States of America

First Warner Books Printing: June, 1990

10 9 8 7 6 5 4 3 2 1

to my parents

SHADOW
TIGER

1

THE TIGER PAUSED for a moment in a doorway and watched the entrance to the hotel on the other side of the crowded street. He was conscious of the weight of a pistol against his leg, and he glanced down, making sure the otherwise empty briefcase was open, the gun quickly accessible.

There were more people on the street than he would like—far more than he remembered would be about at this time of day. Saigon had become a crowded, dirty city, packed with refugees from the North and from the fighting in the surrounding countryside. On the other hand, the crowds would make it harder for anyone to follow him.

He looked around one more time. In spite of himself, the Tiger felt excited, his heart starting to beat faster, a trickle of sweat creeping down his ribs. Now it would begin. He almost smiled. Everything starts with a thought, perhaps even the world itself.

He made his way across the street through the never-ending stream of traffic and stepped between the row of covered stalls. From a distance, a Westerner would not notice anything unusual about him: just another Vietnamese businessman—Western suit, briefcase, and dark glasses, a little taller than average for his race, perhaps, with a more self-assured stride and confident air. Someone, you might say, who knew his way around the cafés and government offices where the big deals were arranged. A man who would know—only too well—the uses of the bribe, the *cua hoi-lo*, and the benefits of influence and family position.

But the Vietnamese could tell. The walk, the set of the shoulders, the arrangement of his features, the almost undefinable differences that amounted to an insurmountable barrier. A *Tay lai*, they would whisper, a mixed blood. A Viet contaminated by the French. *Lai*, the same word with a slightly different pronunciation could mean a mongrel horse or sexual relations.

In the dimness of the hotel bar, the Tiger barely glanced around before he sat down at a vacant table. He did not remove his dark glasses. The emaciated-looking barman came up and set down a drink in front of him before quickly moving away.

The bar seemed only slightly cooler than the street. It was a small place, with cramped plastic tables, chrome-legged chairs, and a large fan that circled sluggishly in the center of the ceiling. A short flight of steps led up to the hotel lobby, where there was constant movement and laughter. On the steps, a small boy sat with a brush and pan. The barman shouted at him angrily, and the boy scrambled away. Somewhere there was a low, erratic hum of an air conditioner in need of maintenance.

All the customers were Vietnamese except for one: Sitting alone at the bar, looking at his reflection in the mirror behind the stacked glasses and clustered bottles, was the American. He was easy to spot.

Outside, a mass of people flowed past in the dense marsh heat. Laughing, shoving, the crowd moved like a tide, spilling into the roadway and eddying around the stalls that sold dried meat, sugarcane juice, rice, and dozens of other things. On the other side of the street, the Tiger could see ornate, three-story buildings with metal railings around balconies on the upper floors. Everywhere there were flapping signs and banners. There was a heavy sprinkling of uniforms among the crowd, but most of the men wore black pants and loose white shirts. Women fluttered along in traditional tight-fitting dresses and silk trousers. Robed monks with shaven heads walked slowly, like islands of tranquility in the seething ebb and flow of the crowded sidewalks. Motor scooters and low-slung sedans, mostly Renaults and Citroens, honked their way past, while there was a constant flow of bicycles, pedicabs, and small taxis with high-pitched, whining motors. Through the open doorway, the noise was a constant hubbub. The river was not far away, and a heavy odor hung in the air, a mixture of stagnant water, fuel oil, dead fish, and algae.

Saigon. The seat of the mandarinate. To most Vietnamese in the South, it was the source of repression: levies, taxes, compulsory induction into the military. The Tiger watched an old man pass the doorway, slow and dreamlike, an opium addict, little more than a walking spinal column. A group of soldiers pushed past, laughing at the old man. The South's army had adopted American uniforms and rank insignia. More proof of the subservience of the Saigon regime to its American masters.

They are like the French, mused the Tiger, they have lost the will of Heaven. And he who departs from Heaven's will is wrong. He was pleased with the thought. Confucianism was not officially recognized in the North, but it showed the Tiger's Vietnamese roots. His gaze wandered around the room, his face impassive and expressionless.

The American was staring out into the street. He was a tall, thin man, in his late thirties, dressed in an ill-fitting suit of some synthetic material, his hair neat and short. Now he stirred uneasily on his stool and glanced furtively at his watch, as if waiting for someone and growing impatient. The Tiger could guess what he was thinking. The American did not like being here in a Vietnamese hotel bar. It made him feel exposed and alone, an obvious foreigner, sitting in the oppressive heat. His shirt was sticking to his back, and he looked tired, probably from constant tension and overwork.

"Would you have a light, sir?"

The Tiger's English was good, almost unaccented, precise. The American looked up, startled. It was the well-dressed Vietnamese he had noticed stroll in a short while ago and had put down as a businessman looking for a black-market contact. The Tiger leaned his briefcase against the bar.

"Sorry, no. I—er—don't smoke. Too young." The American smiled awkwardly. You were never sure how much English these people knew. Surprisingly, the other man laughed. He took out a cigarette case—silver, with a deeply etched design—and pushed the cigarette back into it.

"Then I must find a white-haired grandfather."

The Tiger sat down on a stool next to the American.

"You are here on business, Mr.—?"

"Bob Davis. I sell business machines. Calculators. Typewriters. Dictation equipment. You name it. We also have a new line of digital readout instruments. The latest thing."

The American had a nervous gesture of raising his chin in a jerky motion, stretching his neck to clear his shirt collar.

"Interesting," said the Tiger. "It is true what they say about Yankee ingenuity. Let me buy you another beer."

He signaled the barman.

The American looked uncomfortable. It was obvious that he wanted to be alone. He glanced at his watch again, but the Vietnamese seemed not to notice.

"And what company are you with, Mr. Davis?" The Tiger's eyes were remote behind his glasses. The American stared back at the Vietnamese, trying to see his eyes, something that would give definition to the features.

"Milton Business Machines, Los Angeles," he said with the enthusiasm of a salesman. "We've been in business for about seven years. We've also got offices on the East Coast and in Dallas."

"And now in Saigon," said the Tiger. His smile made him look different somehow from other Vietnamese, someone not quite Oriental.

"Yes, well, with the war here and a stronger American presence, it's opened up great marketing opportunities. There're opportunities all over Southeast Asia. This is going to be one of the best markets in the world. Better than Europe." The American paused, examining the Vietnamese closely. "Are you connected with the military or the government? Your English is very good."

"I learned my English a long time ago. When there was another war here. Some of us would say it is all the same war."

The American was quiet for a moment, thinking hard. The Vietnamese was older than he had first assumed. Up close, he could see the flecks of gray in his hair. The face was hard-looking, tough, but smooth and hairless.

"It is interesting what you say about opportunities, Mr. Davis. Are all opportunities the same everywhere in Asia?"

"Well, politics is not my line," the American replied easily. "I just sell business machines. But I think we're doing the right thing here. Maintaining this as part of the Free World. Without us—I mean, without all of us pulling together—the whole of Southeast Asia could fall to the Communists. That's what Eisenhower said. All these countries could fall like dominoes."

The Vietnamese said nothing, staring in the mirror behind the bar. The will of Heaven.

The American looked around uneasily. It was getting

darker outside. An afternoon thunderstorm. One of the bar patrons, a thin man with bushy hair, had stood up and was looking out of the window. The American moved uncomfortably on the stool. He was sweating. His arm nudged the lightweight .38 he had holstered under his coat.

"And your country will prevent this, Mr. Davis."

It was hard to tell if it was a question or a statement.

"If not us, who?" said the American. The neck squirmed above the wet collar.

The Tiger nodded slowly and tapped the bar with his fingers. He smiled at the mirror.

"You are waiting for someone, Mr. Davis?"

The American looked up almost guiltily from his wristwatch.

"Yes. Yes, I'm waiting for a friend."

The man with the bushy hair had now moved to the door and was looking up and down the street.

"I didn't catch your name," said the American. His face was shiny with sweat.

The Tiger turned and looked at him steadily. He seemed not to hear the question.

"Why are you in Saigon, Mr. Davis?"

"I told you. Business machines."

The American looked around again quickly. Something was very wrong. The barman was down at the other end of the bar working at something under the counter. The movement of the crowd outside seemed to pick up momentum as if sensing the coming rain. Thunder rumbled in the distance. The hawkers were covering up their stalls, laughing as they shouted to each other. A nimble Chinese maid trotted past, wearing black silk trousers and a pale blue jacket, hair plaited in a single braid, an umbrella clutched in a golden hand. Several of the customers had drifted out. The others talked quietly, their heads together, or stared out of the window impassively.

The American saw that the man by the door was staring at him. He moved his hand toward his belt.

"In these times, no one can be sure," the Tiger said quietly. He moved slowly, leaning forward, one arm hidden.

But the American was distracted, looking from side to side, his expression worried. He had been brought to the bar by a message delivered by a Vietnamese police detective, someone he had never seen before. It was urgent for him to meet his Surete contact, a man with the code name Ash, right away. The North had sent someone down. A new man. Someone who was ordered to perform special missions in the city. It was the choice of meeting place that made it all wrong. Usually, he met Ash in a bar near the American Embassy where there were plenty of Americans or out at Military Assistance Command, Vietnam headquarters at Tan Son Nhut Airport. But this was all wrong. With a sickening sense of dread, he realized it now.

The air seemed heavier, stifling, making breathing difficult; the rotting smell of vegetation from the river, stronger.

The man in the doorway was gone.

The rain suddenly hissed down, and a group of giggling girls ran past, holding packages over their heads. In the bar and hotel lobby, all conversation ceased, movement stopped, as if suspended by the outside torrent.

The American stood up. He looked down at the floor, the doorway, then the floor, as though measuring the distance.

"Are you going, Dr. Ewald?" said the Tiger. In the sudden gloom, his eyes were lost behind the glasses.

"Ewald? You've got it wrong. My name's Dave—Davis."

The American took a step toward the door, hand fumbling under his jacket. There was a sudden crack of thunder. Outside, the pavement gleamed wetly. An old Citroen, packed with Vietnamese, splashed past.

"You are Lawrence Ewald from the State University of Michigan," said the Tiger, his voice distant, quiet, as if he were talking gently to a child. "You are with the United States Embassy, and you do classified police work for the Diem government and your own intelligence service."

The American turned quickly, but the Tiger already had a pistol in his hand. It was a Japanese Nambu, and the U.S. adviser stared at it with surprise, as if noticing the make at this moment was something extraordinary. He groped inside his jacket for the .38, his movements tired, much too slow. Ewald never even had his gun in his hand before the Vietnamese fired. The crash was tremendous in the small room.

The man to whom the North Vietnamese had given the name Tiger walked over to where Ewald lay on the floor, crumpled against the front wall. He knelt and carefully removed the American's wallet, passport, and papers. Already blood was spreading across Ewald's shirtfront, welling out of a large wound in his chest. The American moaned and stared up at the ceiling.

The Tiger scanned the papers briefly and then pushed them into his pocket. Ewald's hand flopped tiredly on the floor. His mouth opened, as if trying to say something.

"You should have stayed in Michigan, Dr. Ewald," the Tiger said almost gently. He stood up and leveled the gun at Ewald's head. The American closed his eyes. To the other patrons huddled under the tables the second shot seemed even louder than the first.

The Tiger returned the pistol to the briefcase and looked down at the body of the American. This was going to set the pattern to the rest of his life. A resolved course of action that would inevitably lead, and of this he was certain, to an ending that was already predestined. As if the events had been set in place and only needed this moment to begin the ticking of the clock. Without a backward look, the Tiger briskly walked out into the pouring rain.

2

THE THREE MEN said little to each other as they sat facing the empty desk in the deputy director's spacious office on the third floor of the CIA building near Washington. The deputy director was late, and they looked at each other uncomfortably as if they were strangers who had suddenly been thrown together at a party after hurried introductions by the host.

Al Schofield shuffled some papers on his lap absently and then put his head back, gazing up at the ceiling. He had been out sailing his boat that weekend, the second man, Felix Corman, noticed; there was a bad burn on Schofield's forehead where his hair was receding.

The third man in the room was easily the most impressive. Strongly built, in his midfifties, he was dressed in the uniform of an army lieutenant general, and it was adorned with six rows of medal ribbons, a Presidential Citation, a combat infantryman's badge, and pilot's wings. The black name tag pinned to his pocket said Vossenack.

Felix looked down idly at the file he was holding. Vossenack was the one who was going to be difficult.

The deputy director strolled in and, with a "sorry, gentlemen," took his place behind the desk. He crossed his legs and smiled at everyone present, his lean, handsome face glowing with a healthy tan. He was an elegant, tall man, impeccably dressed in a lightweight gray worsted. His shoes, Felix saw, had little tassels on them. Richard Hoyt, Jr., married to an heiress from one of the oldest monied families in the country, as everyone knew, had many irons in the fire. He had come to the Agency from a prominent Washington law firm, one of those institutions where there was constant movement between private and professional life. There was not much that happened in the Agency, or on Capitol Hill for that matter, that he didn't know about, and his friends in politics and business were legion. It was certain that in some administration soon, perhaps even this one, he would be given a cabinet position.

"I must apologize for being late. The director was having one of his fits over the British," said Hoyt.

Schofield and Corman smiled. The current director's anglophobia, derived from an Irish ancestry, was well known.

"Bob, how are you? How's Margaret?" Hoyt said to the general.

"Just fine, Richard."

"Glad you could make it. Congratulations on your confirmation. We must get in a golf game before you leave." The general nodded.

The deputy director swiveled in his chair. "Everyone's been introduced, right?"

There was a murmur of assent.

"Well, we are all here to look at a situation that we have in Saigon. Bud Schack out there tells us that they've hit a wall in finding this—er—"

"Lazar," said Felix.

"Lazar." The deputy director tapped his fingers together and seemed to gaze contemplatively at a wall that held a display of several dozen photographs all in the same type of frame. The deputy director was in all of them. There was the deputy director shaking hands with the president, shaking hands with the director, and shaking hands with various senators. The deputy director grinned with his wife and two daughters at their horse farm near Hagerstown. The deputy director smiled at a British general, talked with the French president, and skied somewhere. Felix knew without seeing them that Hoyt had several similar arrangements on the walls of his Georgetown house and at his farm.

"Felix, give us a rundown on this Lazar once again."

Felix looked down at the folder on his lap. It was Lewis Sanders's file. He didn't open it.

"Lazar is a Eurasian. His father was a mix of French and Tonkinese, while his mother was from the south, probably of Annamese ethnic stock. He was trained to be an administrator in the French colonial government but took to the jungle when the Japanese entered the country during the war." Felix paused. The deputy director was looking at him with intense interest, while General Vossenack appeared to be lost in thought. Schofield still looked up at the ceiling.

"We don't know much about his early life," Felix pressed on. "Apparently, he was married, briefly, in his early twenties to a Vietnamese Catholic, but they later divorced. There's some indication that a child was born just before the war, a daughter, but we don't know for sure. What we do know is that Lazar, somewhere along the line, became a convert to communism. And when he was operating in the jungle, his group was assisted by the OSS team commanded by Lewis Sanders. We know that they became very good friends."

Felix again paused, and then Schofield broke in.

"They did a lot of damage to the Japanese during the war. In fact," he smiled wryly, "we even awarded Lazar a decoration, the Legion of Merit."

"Hah," the deputy director snorted.

"Sanders went into Hanoi with his OSS team—and with Lazar—just after the end of the war. That must have been about"—Felix glanced in the file—"September 1945. We pulled out all our people in October when the situation started to deteriorate and we didn't want to antagonize the French, who, as you know, were very suspicious of our intentions anyway."

"But Sanders," Schofield's voice betrayed his Massachusetts background, "knows Lazar. He knows how Lazar operates. How he thinks. And most importantly of all, he knows what Lazar looks like."

There was silence for a moment. Felix suddenly realized that one of the photographs on the wall showed Hoyt with a well-known singer. The deputy director began to tap his fingers together again.

"Lazar can do us a lot of damage. If he's done what Schack says he's done—and all indications are that he has—then he's good. Very good." Hoyt stirred in his chair and looked at the three men in front of him, then directly at General Vossenack.

"Bob, we have asked Major Sanders to return to the field with carte blanche." He glanced at Schofield. "Carte blanche," he repeated, "to capture or neutralize Lazar any way he can."

"I think that's a mistake." General Vossenack's voice was flat, without regional accent or inflection.

Hoyt nodded as if the general's objection was perfectly reasonable. "We understand you've had some experience in dealing with Sanders, Bob."

"Yes, I was his commanding officer at one point when his special ranger company was assigned to my division. I don't feel that he has the maturity or the ability to handle this assignment or any other that would come under this category." Vossenack looked around at the others aggressively. "Sanders has trouble obeying orders. That sort of individual is unpredictable in any military operation, especially,"—the general paused to emphasize the word—"especially one of this nature. He is also one of those individuals who feels that"—Vossenack seemed to choose his words carefully, and they came out of him with a grimace, as if he they gave him indigestion—"he knows better than his commanding officer, or anyone else for that matter, how a mission should be conducted. Personally, I find that sort of thing intolerable."

"Hm." Hoyt glanced again at Al Schofield, then at Felix. He tapped restlessly on the top of his desk. It was a solid piece of walnut.

"Sanders will be kept under a very tight rein, Bob. You should actually have very little contact with him, once the mission is underway. But, to ensure that Sanders knows, shall we say, where the orders are coming from, we intend to have one of our people with him at all times—who is it again?"

"David McWaters, lieutenant, junior grade," said Felix.

"Oh yes, a navy man. Must be wondering what the hell he's got himself into by now."

"He's young, but we think he can do the job for us." Schofield scratched again at his burn.

Vossenack stirred in resigned agitation. Antagonizing the CIA was not the best way to start an assignment as ambassador to South Vietnam. He capitulated.

"Okay. But I insist that very close controls be kept on this entire operation. And I, for one, intend to do just that." It was a weak protest, and he and everyone else in the room knew it.

"We appreciate your concern, Bob," said the deputy director smoothly, "and I assure you that everything possible will be done to avoid problems that might be caused by . . . ah, Major Sanders's predisposition toward . . . ah, unauthorized behavior. Any more questions?" There was silence. "Righto. Al, let's go with the operation. And I want to see the budget on this." The deputy director liked to use Britishisms. Some said it dated from the time he was station chief in London, while others said he merely used them to annoy the director.

The conference broke up quickly, with murmurs about other meetings and congratulations to Vossenack.

"Bob, let me walk you out," said Hoyt. Outside the office, the conversation and the deputy director's laughter died away down the hall. Felix weighed Sanders's file in his hand, as if sensing the presence of the tough, resilient man he had recently talked to one afternoon in the California foothills—and he felt a sense of discomfort, almost an embarrassment, as if he had betrayed a friend. But this was impossible, he told himself, because Sanders was someone he barely knew.

"The Central Committee appreciates your work and sends you greetings, comrade commissar," said the comrade general. He was a wizened man with a stooped back, one shoulder slightly higher than the other, the result of a French mortar shell in 1952. The comrade general had once loaded ships on the Haiphong docks, Lazar remembered. He sat now on a stool, wearing a sandy green uniform, and it was hard to think that this little man had helped defeat the generals of France, officers who had been steeped in the traditions of Napoleon at St. Cyr.

"Please convey my thanks to the Committee, comrade general."

They sat drinking green tea from metal cups in Lazar's jungle headquarters, a low bunker made of logs and earth with branches laid across the roof as camouflage. As a concession to his rank—the political commissar had equal authority with military commanders—there was a piece of canvas draped across the door for privacy. The area in front of the bunker had been cleared of vegetation so that snakes would be visible, including the deadly *cham quap*, a small brown krait that resembled a stick and was almost indistinguishable from dry foliage on the ground. The bunker was a few yards from one of the entrances to an intricate system of tunnels that were the headquarters for Battalion D-608 of the People's Liberation Army of Military Region IV. The complex was just north of Cu Chi, about twenty-five miles from Saigon, in an area the Americans would later call the Iron Triangle. In the early sixties, the Vietcong had not moved their operations entirely underground in this area, as they later did.

The general sat silently for a moment, as if savoring the taste of the liquid. He was a deliberate man, who liked to take his time—patient like a spider, they said, and the analogy seemed to fit his small twisted frame. He was an old revolutionary, close to Giap, and this power made him a man one listened to carefully—and a man to fear. Lazar had first met him in 1944, when Lazar had gone into the jungle to fight the Japanese. The Vietminh had welcomed him gladly in those days, as they did anyone with the skills and knowledge shown by an education at a French convent school and admittance to the colonial civil service. The comrade general had been the commissar in Lazar's guerrilla group—and the man who had taught him, had shown him the profound logic of communism as the only course for a new Vietnam. It was the comrade general who had induced him to read Lenin's *Thesis on the National and Colonial Questions*, the essay that had swayed Ho Chi Minh himself.

"I'm delighted to report that the Committee approves your project and has every confidence that your mission will be successful. While our resources are presently limited in the south, of course, it places whatever we have at your disposal." The canvas door had been pulled back and the general gazed out at the jungle. Beyond a roofed-over kitchen with stoves made from gasoline drums, there was a small clearing. A file of black-clad guerrillas walked past. They were carrying a mixture of French and American weapons, some of them handmade copies. Cooks were preparing a meal. The Vietcong, always starved for protein, ate anything—wild dogs, monkeys, even elephants and jungle moths—to supplement their few chickens and pigs.

A group of entertainers, three men and two young women from the North, were practicing for a show that evening, the sound of their singing and laughter incongruous in the jungle setting. As the Saigon government had neglected traditional Vietnamese arts, so the National Liberation Front emphasized them, another tool to win over the hearts of the populace. Further away there was the noise of hammering and somewhere someone was trying to start an engine.

"We prefer that you maintain discretion and keep knowledge of your mission to as few as possible. You will not inform the representatives of the Party Regional Committee for *Trung Bo*."

Lazar's face was blank. His mission was important. Not even the local NLF cadres were to have any knowledge of it.

The comrade general was gazing into the distance. "You have done very well, Jai. You have come a long way in the Party for someone with your background." Lazar's face was stony. Always the reference to his mixed ancestry—sometimes subtle, sometimes more overt, as now. There was always the hint, the few words that reminded him of his blood tainted with that of the hated colonizer. It was more, he knew, than the xenophobia of the Vietnamese: it was the shame that he forever carried with him. He sometimes wondered if his assignment to the front in the South was not a reward, but some form of abstruse discrimination.

"You have earned the trust we place in you, Jai. We

will not forget you." The general sipped his tea delicately. "One day soon, after your mission has been successfully accomplished, you will return to Hanoi for a more fitting post."

"I appreciate the Committee's faith in my work," said Lazar. "The comrade general will perhaps remember that I have applied for an overseas post. Perhaps with an embassy..."

"There are difficulties with such assignments, Jai. But we will see, perhaps something can be done."

"Very well, comrade general."

The general sighed and looked around the small room. It was almost bare except for a rope bed, some books and a spare set of black pajamas on a shelf fixed between two poles, a few chairs, and a rickety table. Laying on the table, carefully oiled, was an AK-47, a weapon worth its weight in gold to the VC. There was also a transistor radio, one of hundreds donated to the People's Liberation Army by the Japanese Communist Party. The relentless spread of Japanese technology, thought the general. A map was pinned to a sheet of canvas attached to the log wall. "One day the war will be over, Jai. Patience. That is something the Americans don't have. One day we will win because we have outlasted them."

He finished his tea and stood up. Jai came to his feet. The comrade general was returning to Hanoi.

"I'll leave while there's still light." The general picked up his sun helmet from the table and looked at Lazar for a moment. The first time their eyes had met since the meeting began. The general's eyes had a yellowish tinge, and Lazar remembered that he suffered from attacks of malaria. What was there in his mind? Lazar thought. What feelings were still buried deep? What hopes, what ambitions? Had it all been wrung out of a man who had been imprisoned for years, who had fought one enemy or another all his life, whose own wife and son had died in a French jail?

"Good luck, comrade Tiger," said the general.

He turned abruptly and walked out.

Lazar sat down again and lit a cigarette. Outside, the engine had finally been started. A group of soldiers was forming in the clearing for the evening parade. He would be expected to go out and read something to them. Current orders. Encouragement from their comrades in the North. The words of Ho and Giap. No single guerrilla of the Vietcong was to have the slightest doubt about the reasons why he or she was fighting. Mao had written, "The basis for guerrilla discipline must be the individual conscience." No one could force a man or woman to be a guerrilla. Motivation was the key. Without knowing that they were engaged in a heroic struggle to liberate the motherland, the hardships and dangers of guerrilla life would be unendurable.

Lazar picked up a pamphlet and the latest directive from the Regional Committee. He had not told everything to the general. He thought about his last meeting with the police detective Luong. They had met in a narrow room above a stinking canal in the Cholon Chinese district of Saigon. The room belonged to a prostitute, an opium addict, who sat in a corner nursing a baby. The detective's face had shone with sweat as he had told Lazar about Ewald, his habits, what he looked like, what he did for the South Vietnamese.

Lazar had listened, noting everything the nervous policeman did, every twitch, every gesture of his shaking hand. The policeman was committing treason. Only his parents, Catholics, in the North were the fulcrum on which his commitment to the revolutionary cause rested. Lazar had listened, and then he had started to question, slowly for several hours, going over details, motives, reasons. And when he had learned all he could about

Ewald, he had more questions. About MACV headquarters and the U.S. Embassy. They went over procedures, methods, security arrangements. The people who worked there. How many Vietnamese? How many Americans? The new ambassador who was due to arrive. The vehicles they used. He had questioned the sweating detective far into the night, trying not to reveal too much of his motives or a hint of what he had in mind. But Lazar knew that Luong was clever enough to get the idea that the Eurasian was planning something big, some gigantic act that would stagger both the Diem regime and America's commitment to it.

He had not been able to get Luong out of Saigon fast enough after he had killed the American adviser. The South Vietnamese had collared the renegade detective in a roadblock as he was trying to make his way across the bridge over the Kinh Ben, the canal-like river south of the city. Luong would have been tortured before being shot—that was certain. And he would have told all he knew about Lazar—that also was certain. But what would the South Vietnamese and the Americans find out? Only that he was planning something. He had divulged no hint, not the slightest indication of what he was thinking. Lazar thought this over carefully. No, there was no way the Americans could know what he was going to do. Bu they were intelligent enough to know that he was going to do something, and they would send someone to get him. A hard man, someone like him. But he would strike first, and when he did, the American resolve in Vietnam would be shattered.

Lazar stood up, straightening his black uniform with the sewn-on tabs of a major. It seemed to fit him better than it did most officers in the People's Army. He was always a neat, tidy man. Orders were being shouted outside. The battalion commander and his staff were waiting for him. Lazar took a soft cap from a peg and then seemed to pause as if remembering something. He was as Vietnamese as they were. His grandfather, that imperialist bastard from France, was an aberration, a distortion in his past. Lazar glanced at his bag of personal effects on the shelf. No one, not the comrade general or anyone in the Central Committee, knew what he carried in that bag. Nobody knew that in it was an old and creased photograph. It showed his grandfather in his uniform, an *adjutant* in the French Army. Lazar would take it out secretly and look at it once in a while. And perhaps the comrade general would have had other, more disconcerting thoughts about the comrade commissar if he had known that one of Lazar's dearest memories was of a gruff, white-mustached old man, who had sung French songs as he held Jai on his knee, had fed Jai cakes and sweets, and had loved the boy very much.

3

"It's not the best of accommodations, but it serves. You'll be here for three or four days. Most of the time you'll be doing physical conditioning and using the rifle ranges. We'll be briefing you in the evenings. There's not much time to go sight-seeing, but you probably know this area, anyway. You did some training here during Korea, didn't you?"

Lewis Sanders had his back to the young navy lieutenant, looking out through the dusty window of the small cadre room.

The room had a bunk made up with a green army blanket, a chair, and a plywood closet. His small suitcase stood on the floor, looking incongruous in such a military setting. It was real leather but had seen a lot of use, McWaters noticed.

They were in a remote part of Fort Ord known as the East Garrison, a scruffy collection of yellowish brown warehouses and unused two-story barracks, like the one they were in now. An old cavalry post, not used for anything these days except storing broken desks and the M-1 rifles they were phasing out and, fenced in down by the dirt road, a truck motor pool.

"No, I was at Devens." Sanders turned from the window.

The voice was low and gravelly. When Sanders turned, McWaters saw it belonged to a stocky man, about average height but who looked shorter, with wide hefty shoulders like a linebacker. Sanders stood with legs apart, the knees slightly bent as though he was ready to meet a charge or make a sudden move. What was most impressive was his head. It was large, almost too large for his body. Heavily tanned, the face was rugged, what society writers and those who follow politicians and film stars call craggy, the features heavy and pockmarked. If you looked closely, a jagged scar, still pink and white around the edges, extended from the side of his neck to somewhere on his chest. In contrast to his deep tan, the man's eyes were a startling blue, clear and with an almost detached expression. A stiff shock of graying hair fell over his forehead. He was dressed in a tan suit, tieless, with his white shirt open several buttons down, and he wore dark brown cowboy boots.

Felix, who was sharing another room with McWaters at the other end of the building, came in and nodded to the young lieutenant, who was holding a clipboard and pen at the ready. The CIA man dropped a pair of boots on the floor and tossed a set of army fatigues on the bed.

"These should fit." He grinned at Sanders. "Must seem like old times. When would you like to get started?"

Sanders took off his jacket and put it carefully on a wire coat hanger in the closet.

The instructor was a thin black staff sergeant with a look of perpetual anger and the name Towner stenciled on the white tape sewn over the pocket of his well-starched fatigues.

He looked Sanders over closely and evidently didn't like what he saw.

"When ah say move you gonna move," he said by way of greeting, and then added, "sir."

They did a lot of running that first day, with the sergeant hurrying Sanders along by firing exploding shells at him from a short fat pistol. The sergeant had it down to an art, and the shells would land right behind Sanders as he staggered up hillsides, exploding with a loud harmless bang, but occasionally he felt a sharp sting as he was peppered with the fragmented aluminum case. They seldom saw or met anyone, but in the distance Sanders could hear firing from the rifle ranges where draftees were training.

Unarmed combat was a series of sudden sharp encounters with the sergeant that left the soldier with a bloody nose and Sanders spreadeagled on the grass gasping for breath. The sergeant, a young man in his twenties, looked at Sanders with more respect.

"Ah kin see you've done this befo'—sir," he said, wiping away the blood with a dirty khaki handkerchief. The sergeant was laying the dialect on thickly.

Felix and McWaters, watching from a distance, glanced at each other with satisfaction.

"He's still in pretty good shape," McWaters said. "He must be—what—in his forties by now."

Felix smiled.

"I understand he got a lung wound way back. How did he get it?"

"Korea. He was leading a ranger company that operated behind the enemy lines for some period—special targets, that sort of thing." Felix blinked in the bright hazy sunlight. Somehow it still seemed chilly. The ocean was no more than a half-mile away. "Some of those missions were under our direction. Later on, his company was more directly under army control and attached to a regular infantry division. Sanders was conducting an operation behind North Korean lines when the Chinese Communists attacked across the Yalu in nineteen-fifty. He was wounded attempting to lead his company to safety."

McWaters shook his head as if this was all ancient

history, and for someone who was not even in high school when it happened, perhaps it was.

"Remarkable," said the lieutenant. And Felix suddenly felt old. He put up the collar of his jacket. Even though the wind was cold the sun was burning into his skin. He glanced around for some shade, but apart from a few stunted oak trees in the distance, there was none.

"What's the story on his daughter?"

Felix jabbed at some ice plant with his foot. "She's autistic," he said. "In a special school in Iowa. She's twelve."

On a firing range built on the sand dunes near the ocean, Sanders tried out various weapons, firing at distant paper targets until they were obscured by the chill evening fog drifting in from the Monterey Bay. Meals were brought out to them by truck from some mess hall in the main part of the complex. The driver ladled out the food from large pots onto steel trays and then sat inside the cab watching curiously as they ate in silence.

In the evening, Sanders joined Felix and McWaters in their cadre room.

"We know that Lazar is behind the killing of several of our people in recent months." Felix rummaged in his suitcase for some sunburn cream. He put some on his nose, peering into a mirror nailed to the wall. "We understand that he was the one who killed a police administrator of ours named Ewald, about a month ago. We sweated the information out of a police detective named Ash who was working with Ewald and set him up."

"Ash?"

Felix smiled apologetically. "A code name. We're using trees. His real name is—was, Luong Van Kha."

"Christ."

"Anyway," Felix went on. The sunburn cream was a

white smear on his face. "According to our information, Lazar is working on something big—something we don't know anything about."

"Where did you get this information?"

"The South Vietnamese National Police, the Surete. They wrung it out of Ash—Luong, but we still think it's reliable."

"What else do the South Vietnamese have on Lazar?" Sanders was drinking beer—his fourth, McWaters noticed.

"From what we get from our sources, very little. Some bio data, an old newspaper photograph that you couldn't recognize anyone from. That's about it."

Felix went on to describe the structure of the U.S. Army command in South Vietnam, and then, very carefully, went into detail on how Sanders would operate.

"You'll report initially to our new ambassador when you get to Saigon. You may remember him, Robert Vossenack."

Sanders stared, memories flooding back.

"What!"

"I know you don't like each other after your—er—experience in Korea, but Bud Schack, who heads our department in the Saigon Military Mission, is retiring and coming home. Until we get someone else out there, we felt that it would be logical for you to report to the ambassador temporarily—he's head of our 'country team,' anyway."

Sanders sat thinking hard, barely listening to Felix describe the details on how he would operate.

"You'll fly out on an Air Force transport from Hamilton Air Force Base," the CIA man said. "You can wear civilian clothes or uniform, it doesn't matter . . ."

Sanders listened in silence for a while. Finally, he interrupted Felix, who had launched into an explanation of how Sanders would relate to MACV operations.

"No way."

"What?"

"I said no way. I go out there on my own. I fly out on a civilian aircraft by way of Tokyo. Get me a passport and visa."

"Goddammit, Lew. It's a little late for that and it makes no sense. Why can't you get there the easy way the same as everyone else?"

"Because," Sanders glared at them angrily, "we do this my way or the deal's off. If I'm going into something like this I call the shots—let's get that straight. And another thing," he went on, "I don't care how McWaters here gets to Vietnam, but he's not coming with me."

Felix stared back at Sanders, baffled and annoyed. McWaters fumbled with his clipboard, red with angry embarrassment.

"Okay, Lew," said Felix at last. "We'll do it your way. Dave, have the army fly you up to San Francisco tomorrow morning early and take care of the passport, visa, and a PanAm ticket. Put an Urgent on it. Don't let the local PanAm people give you any flak. Just tell them to get through to Sherwood in New York. You can meet us at San Francisco Airport on Friday. Give me a call when you've got a time." He sighed. "It's your funeral, Lew."

"I know," said Sanders.

The following day Sanders and the black sergeant ran together along dusty dirt roads that wound between patches of ice plant and stunted oak trees.

"What they gonna do with you, man?" said the sergeant.

"They're sending me somewhere to kill someone," said Sanders.

"She-it, man, you could've stayed in Baltimore and done that."

"How do you know that's not where they're sending me?"

"She-it. Wouldn't surprise me what those fuckers did."

Sanders and Felix sat drinking from a bottle of Jim Beam. It was raining, one of those downpours that make you wonder why California is such a dry state. Streaks of water furrowed down the dirty windows of the cadre room.

"Early rain for this part of the country." Felix was drinking to be sociable. He did not really like bourbon.

Sanders grunted. This was already his third drink.

"Do you have a family, Felix?—no, let me guess. You have a good-looking wife, two kids, a dog—probably a setter—and a house in Chevy Chase. Your wife is a gracious hostess, and she belongs to the Women's League." Sanders slumped in his chair, his rough-hewn face starkly lit by the single lightbulb that dangled from the ceiling.

Felix smiled. "Close enough. The dog's a collie."

He was a big man with frank, open features who dressed very Ivy League, like a businessman who had gone to a good school.

Sanders poured himself another drink. "I want you to do one thing for me, Felix."

"Sure."

"I want you to make sure my kid's alright. You know, that she gets the insurance money. That's important. Also I want you to let my wife—my ex-wife—know if, you know, if anything happens."

"Certainly, Lew. The Agency will take care of things. You know that." Felix looked down into his glass. "She lives in Greenwich, Connecticut, doesn't she?"

"Right. Her name's Elizabeth. Elizabeth DeCourt."

"What went wrong with it?" A quiet question.

"Oh, different types of people, I guess. It was a wartime marriage. We met in Washington in nineteen-forty-four, just before I went overseas. She was doing cryptoanalysis for the navy. We just had different views about things and after the war, well, we never did find a compromise. I liked the West, she liked the East. Me going back into the army during Korea didn't help matters. And then we found my daughter had—she had this problem of hers. We couldn't seem to mesh after that. Just a lot of bickering."

Felix looked at the heavy, tired-looking man. He wanted to say something, but he could find no words of comfort.

"I'm sorry, Lew."

Sanders suddenly sat up and swallowed the rest of his whisky.

"Never be sorry," he said.

He stared out of the window. Across the street a cone of light shone down on the corner of a barracks building, but he could see little else except a smeared image that melted into the earth.

He knew that far away in the jungles of Vietnam an old friend had just become his enemy. And he was certain, as sure as he watched the rain-washed moon float across the heavens, that inevitably one of them would die.

It must have been a mistake. Why else would they kill an American who was trying to help them? Lieutenant McWaters, lying on a bed in the BOQ at the San Francisco Presidio, shook his head and went back over the section on Dewey's death. He tried to visualize the OSS major, a twenty-eight-year-old Yale grad, a congressman's son, driving through the streets of Saigon in 1945. A hot, sultry day. An abandoned golf course. Beyond it, the house where the OSS had its headquarters. And then the Vietminh roadblock. Dewey yells something at the

Vietnamese in French. A burst of fire. The major slumps, falls out of the jeep, killed instantly.

McWaters stopped reading and tossed the hurriedly produced DOD directive on the bedside table, his mouth dry. It happened so fast. And, dammit, it was unfair.

Rain rattled against the window. He thought about getting his car and finding a nice bar somewhere. North Beach was loaded with them. But he made no move to get up.

He was a good-looking brown-haired young man, with the easy, confident manner that came from having wealthy parents and the advantages of good schools. He had never lacked for friends or money. Girls had never been a problem for him. He lost his virginity at sixteen, and there had always been a steady parade of willing females since. One day, McWaters was certain, he would be someone important, a leader. But the young man never took these things for granted. He was not jaded by his privileged past or by the greater opportunities that lay ahead. If anything, they held him in awe.

The lieutenant picked up the stapled sheets again and flipped through them. "Our current presence in what was formerly known as Indochina," he read, "probably began with Project Comore in June, 1945. This was a combined American OSS, French, and Vietnamese raid against the headquarters of the Japanese Twenty-second Division at Lang Son. The raid was successful and solidified our presence in the region. The following month a seven-man OSS advance team, code named Deer, parachuted into Ho Chi Minh's camp in the jungle about seventy-five miles southwest of Hanoi . . ." He flipped forward. ". . . the country was then divided according to the Geneva Accords of 1954, with the United States supporting the Emperor Bao Dai as Chief of State in the South and the Communists under Ho Chi Minh in the North. Millions of Catholics chose not to live under

Communist rule and became refugees, resettling in the South. The United States sent a Military Assistance Advisory Group to South Vietnam in 1954, the same year that Ngo Dinh Diem was appointed prime minister . . ."

McWaters tossed aside the material again. From small teams to sixteen thousand advisers. He looked at the window beaded with rain. They had never found Dewey's body. The room had a clammy chill, and he realized suddenly that in all his comfortable life he had never before felt fear.

4

It was a crucial moment. The breath of the five students spurted in the chill air as they studied the master's work intently. The compound was silent, the few sounds muted: a footstep, the faint knock of wood, somewhere the soft sound of dripping water. The master's kimono rustled as he bent over the potter's wheel in concentration. He opened up the hollow clay shape with his left hand. As the tea bowl belled, he put a flat palm and two fingers on the left side of the clay, pushing it slightly so that it was off center, gravity producing an unevenness in the top. The bowl would be fired that way—an imperfection deliberately wrought, a flaw in the beauty, always there as a reminder.

The open workshop, covered with a swaybacked thatched roof held up by a massive blackened beam, was about fifty feet long and twenty feet wide. Inside were long tables covered with piles of unfired pots. To one side was a collection of stoneware jars with wooden lids. Sitting crosslegged on a blue cushion, the master worked at a chestnut handwheel, the object of concentration of the five young men and women sitting around him.

The master worked on, giving no sign that he had noticed Sanders sitting on a bench at the rear of the shop. For an hour, the lesson was taught. Discipline. Control. Beauty.

Several students worked in and around the workshop. The compound covered about an acre, enclosed with a high fence and barred from the street by huge wooden doors with massive iron hinges and bolts. A watchman sat in a small gatehouse reading a newspaper. The ground was covered with flat stone walks and cut logs. Stones formed steps on the inclines, and there were piles of wood here and there to fire the three kilns. Rough wooden tables were scattered about, weathered mouse gray. A student was heating water in a fifty-gallon drum over an open fire, preparing to mix a glaze. Further back in the compound was the master's house, large, with a series of swaybacked thatched roofs and jutting ridge poles. Nearby, Sanders watched one student finish a pot with the careful application of a *kaki* glaze—a deep magenta with a delicate sheen.

It was peaceful here, and Sanders felt strangely relaxed and comfortable, almost happy.

The lesson ended. Students and master bowed. *Sensei* Oyama dipped his hands in a bamboo bowl and wiped them on a towel as the young men and women began other work. He glanced up at Sanders still sitting at the back of the workshop, and then came toward the American smiling.

"Sanders-san."

They bowed to each other and then shook hands. It was as if Sanders had last seen the Japanese yesterday, instead of eighteen years before.

"*Ohayo gozai-masu, sensei*," said Sanders.

The Japanese smiled, and replied in English. "You have not forgotten your Japanese, Lewis. Come, we will have tea."

They went to a small room at the back of the house, and tea was served by a young woman, possibly Oyama's daughter.

They had met in Indochina in 1945. The war was over. The Emperor had broadcast the surrender of Japan to all Japanese forces, and battalions and regiments were parading and stacking arms, more than the few teams of Americans and French on the spot could handle. Sanders still remembered the hot, humid morning near Hanoi. The Japanese major and his battalion stood stiffly at attention, their uniforms clean and pressed, the major somehow even managing to look cool, his crisp white shirt collar neatly outside his uniform coat. Sanders had been conscious of how he and the ragged band of guerrillas standing behind him looked in contrast. Dirty, clothes torn and patched, bandages on wounds and sores. There was sweat running down his back, and already his shirt was wet. Nevertheless, he had stood straight and looked at the Japanese major with something close to pride. They stood facing each other on the parade field.

Stiffly, the Japanese officer had handed over his pistol and sword. Sanders held them awkwardly until Jai Lazar came forward and took them out of his hands. They then saluted each other. The major seemed to be looking at something over Sanders's shoulder, not looking him in the eye.

"Major Oyama, have your men stack arms and assign guards. Then order them to return to their barracks. You will remain here until we receive orders on your repatriation to Japan."

For a moment the major's eyes wavered. They looked at each other as the interpreter, standing to one side, translated Sanders's instructions. This battalion was part of the 227th Regiment, one of the toughest in the Japanese occupation forces. They had found Vietnamese guerrillas staked out with bayonets rammed up their anuses in areas where the 227th operated. Four of Sanders's men had been killed by the 227th. Sanders stared back into the major's brown eyes, and for a moment he had a strange feeling of recognition, that they knew each other, were brothers under the uniform. And then he remembered the bodies, contorted in horrible pain, and he looked away.

The Japanese battalion had gone home, but not its commander. As Sanders and his OSS team waited for instructions near the town of Hoa Binh on the Black River, the Vietnamese, who had operated with them under their Eurasian commander, Lazar, had withdrawn to their own camp. Sanders had expected orders at any moment to move into Hanoi. They had been ordered to maintain good relations with the Vietnamese but to cease any further military operations with them. Nor were they to train or hand over to the Vietnamese any Japanese weapons under American custody. But the Vietnamese had already acquired large quantities of Japanese weapons, as well as French and American arms. They were openly flying their own flag and clashing with the French forces in the area.

The Americans were also surprised to see a few Japanese soldiers training the Vietminh in drill and tactics.

Orders had finally arrived. The Vietnamese Liberation Army was occupying Hanoi despite the opposition of the French. A victory parade was being planned by Ho Chi Minh. Sanders and his team would be part of the American delegation and were to go into Hanoi escorted by Jai Lazar.

When he drove his jeep into the Vietminh camp, guided by a young Vietnamese soldier, Sanders found it larger and more complex than he expected. Squads of black uniformed soldiers were drilling, and he could see others being instructed in weapons handling under large open huts with thatched roofs. Jai Lazar was waiting outside his headquarters hut to greet him, and, to his surprise, the man next to Lazar was Minoru Oyama, still in a clean uniform but without insignia of rank.

Lazar greeted him with his usual enthusiasm. They had worked well together during the fighting. As they shook hands, Sanders had remarked on the presence of Oyama.

"Minoru is extremely helpful to us, Lew," said Lazar. "His experience and training is much too good for us to waste. Soon, however, I am afraid we are going to lose him when he returns to his homeland."

"I'm surprised that you would use someone from the two-hundred-twenty-seventh," said Sanders.

"Soldiers do things in war that are often unacceptable at other times, Captain Sanders," said Oyama, and Sanders was surprised to hear the major speak excellent English. And also, once again, as he regarded the straight-backed officer, he briefly felt the bond.

What happened next surprised everyone. As they talked about the coming victory parade in Hanoi, a black-clad Vietminh soldier suddenly screamed and fired at Oyama. The shot went wild. For a moment the tableau froze, as everyone stood astounded. Then the soldier, wild-eyed and foam flecking his mouth, ran at the Japanese officer with a bayonet-fixed rifle. Oyama, unarmed, swung into a fighting stance. Almost without thinking, Sanders dove for the Vietminh. They both tumbled to the ground, but like lightning the soldier was up again, stabbing at Oyama. He might have been able to evade the bayonet, but as Oyama stepped back he lost his footing and sprawled on the ground. The Vietminh raised his rifle over his head, the bayonet poised, and then the shot rang out and he plowed forward into the ground as if a giant fist had hit him. Men came running. There was a babble of voices. Lazar looked down at the dead man, astonished. Oyama stood up.

"Thank you, my friend. I am in your debt," said the Japanese major. He was brushing himself off, almost casually.

"Forget it," said Sanders. "I was the only one with a weapon handy." He holstered his .45. "I'm sorry, Jai."

The Eurasian shrugged. There was not much any of them could do for the Vietminh guerrilla. He was dead with his rifle still clutched in his hand. They found out later that he'd had a brother, also a guerrilla, who had been killed by the Japanese. Staked out with a bayonet.

Oyama returned to Japan some months later, but by then Sanders had been ordered back to the United States.

He faced Oyama now across the low table. They were sitting on the floor on their legs, Japanese-style. The potter's back was straight, his shoulders square. A white robe showed beneath the dark blue outer kimono that bore the crest of his clan in white, an arrow's feather. Minoru Oyama. One of the most renowned potters in Japan—some called him a national treasure. Flecks of gray were in his crew-cut hair. Apart from that he still looks the way I first saw him on that parade field outside Hanoi, thought Sanders. He must be in his fifties, now.

They drank tea from delicately glazed bowls much like the one Sanders saw being made out in the workshop.

"This glaze," said Sanders. It was a deep red, almost black. "How do you make it?"

"A *mashiko kaki*. It is an iron glaze made from a volcanic stone we get from a village near here. The stone is ground to a powder and then washed many times. It takes a long time to make."

"Beautiful," said Sanders.

"I am delighted my friend enjoys it," said Oyama.

They chatted for a while about pottery, the new Japan, never directly arriving at the real reason for Sanders's visit. By late afternoon the young woman, it really was Oyama's daughter, his youngest, lit some metal lamps. The master's house had no electricity. It was growing chill inside the house and she brought them wool kimonos and started a charcoal fire in a metal grill. She refilled their cups from a black metal kettle and brought them bowls of rice with strips of grilled meat, glancing shyly at the American. Sanders no longer had any feeling in his legs, and Oyama laughed as he stretched them out. Somewhere in the house there was the cry of a baby, which was quickly hushed. Oyama smiled.

"My grandson."

"Minoru," Sanders paused as he ate. The light from a lamp threw the Japanese man's face in stark relief. He seemed like a statue. And for a moment Sanders could feel the heat again of that summer morning, the sweat soaking his shirt, and the decaying humid smell of the jungle. "I am here because I must find someone we both knew during the war. The man whose soldiers you trained. Jai Lazar."

Oyama's face revealed nothing, as though it was carved from mahogany.

"How can I help you, Lewis?"

"You worked with Lazar for a few months at the end of the war. You know the places, the guerrilla bases, he set up. The supply dumps. The workshops. You know where they are in the north. I remember there was also a rumor that you went down to the south with him. And I think you helped him set up some bases there."

The potter was silent.

"Minoru, I've been ordered to find Jai by my government. I have an obligation."

"I understand." The Japanese looked out of a window that overlooked the compound, now receding into darkness. "Lewis," he said. "Once you saved my life—no,"—Sanders had made as if to protest—"it's true. When I first saw you, that day when I surrendered my battalion, I felt you were my brother. I owe you a debt I cannot repay. Years of work I have enjoyed." He gestured as if to take in the compound, the house. "The time to be with my family, my students." He smiled at the American. "I was a good soldier for Japan, Lewis. I hope I have also been a good artist. It is strange, perhaps, to be both an artist and a soldier. But I must tell you. I have loved both. I'll help you, Lewis. Where can we begin?"

For an hour they pored over some maps that Sanders had brought with him. It was if they had gone back eighteen years. Slowly the names became familiar again. They remembered trails they thought they had long forgotten. Villages. Highways. Fields of fire and ambush sites. Once Oyama tapped a spot on a map.

"About here. If he's anywhere in this region, he will be here."

When they had finished, Sanders folded up the maps, his eyes tired and his legs and back aching. He knew where to start. In the morning Oyama walked with him to the gate.

"There was a Japanese poet named Soseki, Lewis. He was much like us in a way. He wrote a *haiku* that I will try to translate. Something like this:

> The winds that blow—
> ask them which leaf on the tree
> will be next to go."

"Yes, I think I can understand that."

They regarded each other for a moment, their breath steaming in the cold air. Already the work was commencing inside the compound, the sound of a wooden mallet, the dull clap of hard clay on stone. The elderly gatekeeper was standing to one side with his cap in his hand. The American and the potter smiled and both bowed slightly. Both knew they would never see each other again.

"A thousand years, Lewis."

"*Sayonara*, Minoru."

Oyama stood watching Sanders walk down a narrow road toward a small town where he would catch a bus for Tokyo. Before he turned a corner, Sanders glanced back and saw the Japanese still standing there, arms at his sides, like a statue.

Sanders was slightly drunk when he caught a JAL flight that night to Saigon. He slept most of the way, his sleep feverish and haunted by dreams of suffocating, drowning in a dense bog in the middle of a dark jungle. Far away, a man—someone he thought he knew but whose face he couldn't see—stood aloof, watching, while nearby a frail and thin woman sat and cried. It was his mother, he realized. He called to her for help, but she shook her head, tears running down her face, and pointed off into the distance where the man stood with folded arms.

5

AMBASSADOR ROBERT VOSSENACK stood by the window of his office on the third floor of the square, concrete U.S. Embassy building in Saigon with a cup of coffee in his hand and an angry look on his face. If they thought he was going to let some amateur cowboy, a washed-up, spaced-out loony from California, ride roughshod around Saigon they were mistaken. It was time to take the matter firmly in hand. *He* alone was responsible for the conduct of American policy in this country, and he was not going to let the CIA or anyone else, even the army, jeopardize his position and his career record. A record of achievement, he was proud to say, that could be compared favorably with that of any senior official both in and out of government in recent times.

Vossenack was getting heavier as he advanced into middle age, but he still looked as if he could go a few rounds of collegiate boxing, which he once did. His prominent ears were accentuated by his military haircut, and when he smiled, which he did rarely, you could see his teeth were badly crooked, the result of a poor childhood and parents who couldn't afford to take their youngest child, or the other three for that matter, to an orthodontist. General Vossenack had made his way up in the world entirely on his own merits. From the time he had won an appointment to West Point he had never looked back, although once in a while he allowed himself to think that he had come a long way from his childhood on a scrabble dirt farm in Missouri and parents who never got past fourth grade.

He reached out and pushed the window—it had bulletproof glass—slightly open. Even though the office was coolly air-conditioned, the ambassador had always felt closed in by air-conditioned buildings. The window was shielded by an ornamental concrete facade that looked decorative but which actually served the utilitarian purpose of preventing grenades or shells from coming through the opening.

He walked back to his desk and looked down at the yellow sheet of paper, a decoded message from Langley. Sanders had given the CIA watchers in Tokyo the slip. He might even be in Saigon this very minute; no one, unbelievably, knew where he was.

Vossenack had warned them. He'd told them what to expect, and the record showed it. No one could blame him there. Sanders. Goddamn cowboy. Vossenack noted with surprise that his hand holding the cup of coffee was trembling slightly. There was a knock on the door, and his secretary walked in carrying a large folder, the overnight messages from Washington. He put the coffee cup down quickly on his desk.

"Thanks, Sue." The secretary's heels tapped their way across the tile floor to the door.

"Oh, Mr. Ambassador, there's a man in the lobby who's waiting to see you. An American who says his name is Sanders. The guards won't let him upstairs until we call down. He looks rather, well, *unkempt*. I would have told you earlier but you were in conference."

Vossenack stared at her for a moment.

"I—er—will see him presently, Sue. I'll buzz when I'm ready."

The ambassador sat at his large Queen Anne desk and looked at the message from Langley. It sat alone on his desk pad as if isolated from the symbols of his existence around it: the two telephones, the folders, the in and out boxes, his nameplate ("U.S. Ambassador Robert B. Vossenack") set off by a pen-and-pencil set and a small plaque, a gift from the staff of his division in Korea. The plaque showed pictures of the Korean national symbol and a division patch. Between these was an inscription that read, "To Major General Robert Vossenack for his outstanding record as commander of the best division in the U.S. Army from the 12th Division headquarters staff." Vossenack's mind wandered to events years ago and more than a thousand miles away. Korea. Sanders, the goddamn cowboy.

Downstairs in the lobby, Sanders slumped in his chair, eyed with resentment by a spit-and-polish marine sergeant who sat behind a small metal desk near the door that led from the lobby to the interior corridors of the embassy. The lobby held two smiling Vietnamese receptionists behind a large circular wooden desk, potted palms, flags, a large wall plaque depicting an American eagle, and another marine guard who stood by the door and watched the constant stream of people in and out the building—embassy workers, businessmen, visiting officials, South Vietnamese officers, diplomats from other embassies, soldiers, and messengers. Most signed the register at the front desk, were badged and quickly whisked away to their appointments or went about their duties. Only Sanders sat there, on a long, thinly padded seat upholstered in a bright turquoise-colored fabric, his legs stretched out, scuffed cowboy boots crossed at the ankles, his eyes half closed, tan suit wrinkled.

The marine sergeant, a young blond man with a shaven head, picked up Sanders's passport again and leafed through it, inspecting the visa stamp closely.

"What did you say you did," he paused, "sir?"

"Farming. I cultivate and prune." Sanders's voice seemed to rumble up from a long way down.

"Cultivate and prune." The sergeant gave an amused glance at the other marine, who looked on, expressionless.

"Sometimes I plant."

"Oh, what d'you plant?"

"Marines. I plant them head down. They don't know the difference."

The sergeant's face went red. Aware of his position in the public lobby, he struggled to control an angry retort. A snarl finally broke from him.

"You—"

But Sanders had looked up, his clear blue eyes had become icy, staring at the sergeant without blinking. The marine subsided into sullen silence.

The minutes ticked by. Sanders seemed to doze. His large head slumped forward on his chest, his stiff hair splashed across his forehead. As he listened to the chatter of Vietnamese secretaries, the hearty laughter of visiting businessmen and embassy bureaucrats, the figure seemed to well up before him. Vossenack. General Robert Vossenack.

On November 1, 1950, Chinese forces, spearheaded by the Sixty-sixth Army, crossed the Yalu River, driving the Americans and South Koreans before them. Four days later, Sanders's ranger company, sent on a mission to reconnoiter the enemy presence near three power plants on the Chongjin River, and now down to sixty-five men, was trying to make its way back to American lines south of the Funchilin Pass.

Carrying many wounded, and immersed in crowds of refugees, the company trudged along a winding dirt-and-gravel road that switchbacked through snow-dusted mountains. Radio contact with the headquarters of the

12th Division was spasmodic. The company's single radio was damaged, and in any case the high mountains disrupted communication. Intermittently, the column would be bracketed by 82 mm rocket fire from the advancing Chinese somewhere in the hills behind them. They had set dozens of fires to conceal their movements, and the sky was obscured by a smoky brown haze. In the distance the Americans heard bugles and shrill whistles.

Sanders hurried to the back of the column, urging his men along. He was worried. Their only way to safety was an immense concrete-and-steel bridge over the Chongchon River. If that was destroyed they would be cut off. Korean women sat beside the road, wailing over a dead child or an old man killed by the rocket fire. Others staggered along under impossibly large bundles. Some of his men, he noticed, were helping the refugees carry their possessions. Several had small children sitting drooped with exhaustion on their shoulders. The smell of burning was in the air.

"Looks bad, Andy," Sanders said as he came up to Lieutenant Andrew Lloyd, his executive officer, standing beside the radio mounted on a jeep. "We've got to go faster."

There were four wounded men piled in the jeep. Two, perhaps three, were already dead.

Lloyd, nursing a bandaged hand, nodded. He was too exhausted to say anything.

"I've got division, sir," said the radioman.

Sanders grabbed the mike.

"Star Hill One this is Star Hill Two. Captain Sanders speaking. We're bogged down with refugees and carrying wounded. We need four hours to get to the river. Repeat, we need four hours."

The voice came back scratchy, fading out.

". . . One. Your orders are to . . . east to Hagaru . . . marine division, over."

"Star Hill One, repeat message. Please repeat message."

There was a boom of explosives in the distance. The operator's voice came in clearer.

". . . Hill One. Repeat. Proceed east to Hagaru. The . . . division is in that area. Do not, repeat, do not continue south."

Sanders stared blankly at the radio.

"Star Hill One. This is Captain Sanders. I want to speak directly to General Vossenack. I have sixty-five men here. We must get over that bridge. We have many badly wounded. They will die without immediate medical attention. There's also a lot of refugees with us. Three hours, just give us three hours, over."

The radio crackled. There was an immense explosion a few hundred yards down the road and everyone instinctively ducked. "Come on. Come on." Sanders gripped the mike, thinking of Vossenack. Relations between the two were strained to the point of rudeness. Sanders's ranger company had been assigned to the division by the Eighth Army, but Vossenack did not like rangers and had tried to use them as a conventional infantry company. When Sanders had come up with the idea of using turncoat North Koreans as a special commando group attached to his unit, Vossenack had vetoed the idea in disgust. Sanders had then tried taking the plan to the Eighth Army directly. When Vossenack heard this, he had called the captain into his office. The interview had been stormy, with the general accusing the captain of disloyalty, and Sanders telling the general that U.S. Army leadership had forgotten the army's guerrilla heritage. Vossenack had almost choked. Red faced, he told Sanders to get out, saying he was not going to be lectured to by a captain, and a civilian one at that. From then on

Sanders's ranger company had been given every dangerous assignment that came along—something for which Sanders blamed himself.

The voice of the division radio operator came on again, the static crackling.

"Star Hill Two this is Star Hill One. . . . orders are to proceed east and join up with the marine division. . . . cannot get over . . . bridge . . . destroyed in thirty minutes. Repeat, proceed east, over."

"Let me speak to General Vossenack." Sanders gripped the mike, seeing an image of the general in front of him. Starched fatigues. A camouflaged cloth ascot. Sitting behind his huge mahogany desk he had the army ship from Tokyo. His "trademark" presentation .45 in a shoulder holster.

"Star Hill One. Negative, Star Hill Two. Your orders . . . make for Hagaru. Out."

Sanders stared down at the radio. The radio operator, bandages showing beneath his fur cap, suddenly gave a choked sob.

"Damn . . . damn."

They all knew, crippled as they were, it could take them as much as twelve hours or more to struggle across the mountains to Hagaru, surrounded by Chinese all the while. Sanders looked down his tired, staggering column.

"Well, Andy. It looks like the general has changed our plans—"

He never heard the 82 mm rockets coming in. There was just an immense ball of red before his eyes and he felt a tremendous blow in the chest, lifting him up higher and higher and as he sank back down into blackness he thought, mechanically, that this is what it was like to die.

But Sanders didn't die. Somehow his company had managed to struggle on over the mountains toward the east, carrying Sanders in a litter. They lost fifteen more men, including Andy Lloyd, before a marine battalion found them.

"Mr. Sanders?"

Sanders woke with a start, beads of sweat channeling down the side of his heavy, pockmarked features.

"What? Who?"

"Mr. Sanders." It was another marine guard. "The ambassador will see you now, sir."

Groggily, Sanders got up and followed him, picking up his passport and stuffing it in his pocket without looking at the marine sergeant.

The starched marine led him onto an elevator and stood watching Sanders silently as they went up. Sanders wiped the sweat from his face with a grimy handkerchief. His legs felt shaky, as if he had climbed a dozen flights of stairs. The marine led him out of the elevator and down a hallway past another guard to a small anteroom where a woman in a print dress with blond upswept hair sat behind a desk. The marine nodded to her and left.

She looked at his appearance dubiously. "Mr. Sanders, I'm Susan Neff, the ambassador's secretary. He'll see you now." She went to a solid walnut door, knocked, and opened it.

"Er, Mr. Sanders, Mr. Ambassador."

Sanders walked in and stood in front of the ambassador's desk. The door closed behind him. Vossenack leaned back in his chair and looked the stocky man up and down with evident distaste, not bothering to ask him to be seated. Finally, Sanders shrugged and sat down. The dislike between the two men was almost a visible force.

"Good god, Major, you look like hell. Where've you been?" said the ambassador finally.

"The hotel I'm staying at doesn't have too many

conveniences, sir." Sanders's voice rumbled without emphasis or inflection.

"You mean you're not staying at the Continental?"

"No, I'm staying at a Chinese hotel."

"A Chi—," Vossenack stared at Sanders as if he had gone out of his mind.

"Well," he gestured toward the message on his desk, "the Agency is in an uproar over losing you in Tokyo. Although they can't say I didn't warn them. I have been against using you, or even having you in this country, from the start. As far as I'm concerned you showed little ability to lead when you were under my command. And from what I can see, matters have not improved." He tapped a long letter opener on his desk. It was in the shape of a miniature bayonet. "I know all about you, Sanders, your divorce, your business failures."

Vossenack paused, giving his words time to sink in, watching for any resentful response, any sign of Sanders's hate for him. But Sanders continued to lounge in his chair, his calm eyes looking at some distant image that only he could see, not moving or saying anything.

"I mean, good lord, just look at yourself. You can't even keep yourself tidy."

Sanders looked back at the ambassador impassively. Vossenack had changed little since he wore a uniform. His thinning hair was combed back tightly with a parting that looked as if it had been drawn with a ruler. His lightweight business suit appeared as if it were made of cardboard and fitted on with snaps. A pristine rectangle of white handkerchief protruded from his top pocket. The suit seemed to make him look stiff and uncomfortable, the sign of a man who was not used to wearing one.

"All right," Vossenack went on resignedly, "the Agency wanted you because you're the only one we have who knows Lazar by sight, but I just want you to know that I still consider you a liability. In fact, I think this whole operation of yours is useless. Lazar will be caught using appropriate police methods. The South Vietnamese military police are scouring the whole city right now. It's just a matter of time."

"Lazar isn't in Saigon." Sanders seemed to be looking off into the distance.

"There you see." The ambassador waved an arm in exasperation. "You've just got here and already you know more than the South Vietnamese themselves. You're incredible, Sanders."

"Lazar is out in the jungle, and I'm going to have to go out after him."

"Nonsense. Lazar can't strike at us from the jungle. He's in the city, somewhere. This whole idea of sneaking through jungles, operating behind enemy lines is a lot of crap. That's why General MacArthur would never allow you OSS people in his theater of operations."

Sanders remembered that Vossenack had spent most of World War Two on MacArthur's staff.

"This Special Forces concept is also nonsense," the ambassador went on, "and I hope the army comes to its senses about it soon. I suppose there's some limited use for reconnaissance-type troops or special commando-type operations, but very limited. The way to destroy the Vietcong is to keep a tight control on the infrastructure of the country. Maintain a strong force and hit the VC hard wherever they show themselves. Armor. Air power. They can't stand up to that."

"The British in Malaya—"

"The British have their way of doing things, we have ours. Let's not forget that, Major. You seem to be another one of those armchair experts."

"I didn't learn anything sitting in a chair, General."

Sanders and Vossenack stared at each other, both realizing once again the intense differences between them.

There was a sudden knock on the door and a woman came in who looked so much like Vossenack's secretary that for a moment Sanders thought they were the same person—the same upswept blond hair, the same type of print dress.

"Oh, sorry dear, I thought you were alone. Sue wasn't outside."

"It's okay, Margaret. This is, er, Major Sanders. My wife."

Sanders stood up awkwardly, nodding at the woman. She looked as though she was about forty, perhaps thirteen years younger than the ambassador, her age betrayed by crows feet around her eyes and several strands of silver in her hair.

The ambassador's wife gave an automatic smile at Sanders and then she looked a little startled when she noticed his disheveled condition.

"I just dropped in to remind you, dear, the Canadian ambassador and his wife and Bud Bailey from Allied-White Construction tonight . . ."

"Oh, yes. Thanks, Margaret."

"It's been a pleasure meeting you, Major. Will you be in Saigon long?"

"Shouldn't be too long." Sanders looked at her steadily.

The ambassador's wife gave another mechanical smile and walked out.

Vossenack glanced at his wristwatch.

"Well, Sanders, I guess I'm going to have to put up with you here in Saigon for a while. The shorter the better, however, for all concerned—both for you and me. McWaters is already here. He's staying at the bachelor officer quarters at MACV. There's one officer with some sense at least. You'll work with him at all times. And," he emphasized the words precisely, "you'll keep me fully informed. As they told you in California, I'm in charge of this operation until the Agency sends out a new station chief, but I'm holding you entirely responsible for its conduct. Now, do you need any assistance? I can get it from MACV."

"Maybe an interpreter, otherwise I'll work alone with McWaters for a while—until I've got a lead on Lazar."

"Suit yourself." Vossenack nodded. The meeting was over.

They didn't shake hands.

As Sanders walked to the door, Vossenack glared after him.

"And remember, Sanders, don't overestimate the capability of the Communists. They may have been able to beat the French, but we won't make the mistakes the French made. This is a different ballgame."

When Sanders left, Vossenack walked to the window again. He stared down at the pedestrians and the traffic passing outside. Bicycled-powered trishaws, old Volkswagen taxis, strange three-wheeled trucks. A hearse went by, a red truck with huge eyes painted on its headlights and bright yellow legs on its fenders. A small pagoda was built on the truck's roof, complete with puffy clouds and a patch of blue sky. Mourners packed a procession of cars that followed slowly. Near the gate to the embassy compound, military policemen patrolled with rifles and carbines at the ready.

He stared down at the scene, hands locked behind his back. He saw Sanders walk out through the gate and walk up the street, picking his way between the knots of people on the sidewalk. Vossenack's eyes followed him as far as he could, hating the stocky figure in the crumpled suit.

There was a gentle knock at the door, and an elderly Vietnamese in a white jacket entered carrying a tray.

"Coffee, *monsieur l'ambassador*."

"Okay, thanks, Hong."

Vossenack continued to stand with his back to the room as the Vietnamese carefully arranged the coffee and hot rolls on the ambassador's desk, meticulously placing the silverware on a white napkin beside the yellow message slip from Langley.

Further up the street toward the Presidential Palace a crowd suddenly gathered. Vossenack saw a splash of saffron. Another demonstration by Buddhist monks. Pedestrians were running. Banners waved above a crowd of supporters. The ambassador could hear the tinny sound of a bullhorn. An army truck went roaring past, disgorging soldiers before it had even stopped. Police were hurriedly placing barricades across the street. Khaki uniforms seemed to ring the demonstration. He saw rifles raised. There were one or two faint cries.

The servant slipped out of the door quietly, so quietly that Vossenack never noticed as he continued to stare down into the street.

6

THE TINY ISLAND was edged with a thin strip of white bordering a narrow girdle of gravelly beach, and all around it was the brilliant sea, colored in deep shades of blue and green, with here and there a swirl of muddy brown. As the Huey got closer, they could see the prison was nothing more than a dozen single-story buildings and a collection of huts. Further back, there was a bare area hacked clear of scrub and trees and cordoned off with a bamboo fence. From the air, they could see what looked like a collection of large brown patches and boxes scattered inside the compound. This was the broadest part of the island and most of it was covered with scrubby trees and grass and a few dense bamboo thickets that grew almost to the water's edge.

The Huey banked sharply, the deafening sound of its engine changing pitch. Sanders, McWaters, and a Vietnamese army sergeant named Nguyen Van Chu, now their interpreter, braced themselves in their metal seats. The helmeted gunner, a smoked visor hiding half his face, signaled that they were landing.

The landing was surprisingly light, and the two Americans and the Vietnamese quickly unbuckled themselves and jumped out, shielding their faces from the dust and gravel kicked up by the swishing rotors. Once on the ground, the heat hit them like a blast furnace, and both Americans were instantly sweating. Sanders's white shirt now looked grubby and his tan pants were heavily wrinkled and creased. McWaters, in contrast, was wearing crisp navy khakis, a silver bar on his collar and cap.

They looked around curiously. The UH-1B had landed in a slight depression so they could not see much except the roofs of one or two buildings. The steady wind carried sand and salt spray but did little to lessen the heat. Behind them was some scrub-covered high ground toward the center of the island. For years, the French had used this place as a prison, and the Diem government was still using it to house terrorists and VC guerrillas—as well as political opponents who had become too outspoken. As they walked toward the buildings, two officers of the Army of the Republic of Vietnam came out to meet them. They were heavyset men for their race, swaggering slightly, dressed in American Army fatigues. The sergeant saluted, and one of the officers said something to him.

"He say they were told we want to look at a prisoner. We should follow them."

They were led toward the fenced-in compound, and for a while the island seemed deserted, as if there were no one else on it except the two officers who had mysteriously appeared like castaways. Then, when they got closer to the larger buildings, they saw several Vietnamese soldiers peering at them out of windows. They must keep prisoners in some of them, Sanders guessed. Possibly interrogation rooms, a barracks.

About a dozen soldiers were wandering around the fenced compound, looking down at the ground or at the small boxes. Then, with a sudden change in the direction of the wind, the smell hit the two Americans. McWaters put his hand over his mouth, gagging. It was a sickening odor of feces, urine, and unwashed bodies. Sanders looked around impassively.

As they walked into the compound, McWaters almost gasped. What they thought were boxes were small bamboo cages and there were men in them. Some were sitting up, others lay without movement on the bare earth. One man lay muttering to himself, encrusted blood covering his head. And now McWaters realized that the strange brown patches he saw from the air were actually pits dug in the soil each covered with a bamboo trellis. He edged toward one and looked down. The pit was about seven or eight feet deep and about six feet square. For a moment he could see nothing, and then something moved. He stared in horror. There were three women in the pit, dressed in the black pajamas of the Vietcong, their faces streaked with dirt and filth, their heads shaved. They stared up at him in silence. One had a bloody welt across her face. McWaters turned and stumbled past two Vietnamese soldiers who were looking at him in amusement, and hurried after Sanders and Chu, who seemed to stride on, unconcerned.

They all stopped before a bamboo cage.

One of the ARVN officers spoke sharply in Vietnamese. "This is man they think can help you," said Chu. "He is deserter from Republic of Vietnam National Army who join Vietcong. Now he *Hoi Chanh*. He want to—ah, what do you say?"

"Defect?"

"Yes, defect to our side."

The Vietnamese officer said something else.

"This man was captured north of Saigon, near Bien Hoa. He may know the area that interest you."

The man inside the cage was short and thickset with bushy hair and ugly lopsided features. One of his eyes was partially closed, and a large oozing sore on his leg showed through his torn pants. He sat propped against the bars, staring back at them sullenly. The officer roared something at him, and he immediately looked down at the ground, but they could still sense the morose hostility.

"Let's take a look at him," said Sanders.

An officer called to a soldier, who ran forward and released a section of the cage that formed a rough door. The soldier reached inside and grabbed the prisoner by the front of his sleeveless undershirt and dragged him out, knocking him down on the ground and taking the opportunity to land a kick on the prisoner's back.

"*Troi oi*," gasped the prisoner.

"Ask him what his name is," said Sanders, who stood with his hands in his pockets as if inspecting an automobile he was thinking of buying.

An exchange took place between Chu and the prisoner, who answered in a sullen mumble.

"His name is Hoang Van Le."

"Ask him why he deserted the army."

Another exchange took place, and for the first time the prisoner became animated, looking aggressively at the two officers, who suddenly seemed to be embarrassed, glancing at each other.

"He deserted because of new law—what is called family law," said Chu, translating with great care. "The law say that men cannot . . . ah, gamble—that is right word?—gamble."

The prisoner broke in with another long explanation.

"He say the law forbid men to go to fortune-teller and to go to the cockfight. There can be no more dancing or . . . ah, beauty contest. Man cannot divorce wife if she is bad wife, and he cannot go with woman he meet in bar."

"What's all that about," muttered McWaters.

"Something I've read. I think he's referring to the new Family Code that was brought in around fifty-eight. It's one of Madame Nhu's ideas. It banned a whole bunch of things that Vietnamese men like to do. Screwing and gambling mainly." Sanders looked at the prisoner with a slight smile.

"Ask him why he now wants to help the South Vietnamese government."

The prisoner suddenly grinned, showing broken, yellow teeth.

"He say it a no-good government but it better than dying in cage," translated Chu without expression, but the two officers looked at the prisoner angrily.

Sanders kicked at the sandy dirt for a moment and then looked around the compound. The wind blew without pause, whipping salty sand around them. A few hundred yards away, between rolling dunes, he could see a brilliant blue patch of sea. Several ARVN soldiers scattered around the compound were watching the Americans, one or two carrying long clubs.

After a moment, he said, "Okay, we'll take him."

Chu and the soldier hauled the prisoner to his feet and McWaters realized that he had trouble standing. They hurried him along. Some of the prisoners in the other cages began yelling, and this annoyed the guards, who went to work with their rifles and clubs. McWaters looked away with disgust as he saw a soldier strike through the bars of a cage with his rifle butt. There was a splatter of blood and the faint crunch of a prisoner's face.

There were sudden shrill screams from the women, and guards shouted down at them. Some of the soldiers picked up rocks and threw them down into the pits. A soldier ran up with a bucket of what looked like yellowish greasy water and threw the mess down into a pit, laughing, and McWaters suddenly realized that there was urine in it.

As they hurried through the gate toward the waiting chopper, McWaters glanced back. The soldiers had pulled a woman from one of the pits. They clustered around. He heard faintly the woman's high-pitched scream, torn away by the wind. He felt he was going to be sick. But Sanders seemed as undisturbed as if he were taking a stroll along a city street somewhere in the States.

"Tell them thanks," said Sanders to Chu, as they scrambled inside the chopper. The two Vietnamese officers saluted and then hurried away as the Huey's engine whirred and coughed and the rotors began to circle faster and faster. They buckled themselves in with Le sitting on the floor. With a sudden jerk the chopper lifted off and banked sharply toward the mainland a few miles away. McWaters, still shaken, looked down at the island dropping away below them.

"Disgusting," he shouted to Sanders above the noise, and then glanced at Chu with embarrassment, but the Vietnamese sergeant did not seem to have heard.

Sanders barely nodded, his eyes sleepy.

"How do we know that the prisoner won't run at the first opportunity?" McWaters shouted.

"Where's he going to run to? Charlie will soon hear that he's gone over to us. The government police will shoot him on sight. Anyway, we'll have Chu keep a close eye on him." Sanders watched green waterlogged paddies and shell craters filled with brown water appear below them. A narrow asphalted road led off into the jungle. They were rapidly approaching Tan Son Nhut Airport, and he could see the spired pagodas and palaces of Saigon in the distance. Out of the opposite door he looked toward the north. It won't be long, Jai, he thought. I'm coming, buddy boy.

The two Vietnamese generals, one in a white suit, the other in a uniform gleaming with medal ribbons and insignia, sat stiffly but maintained serene smiles across the room at Vossenack.

They were in the small sitting room connected to the ambassador's office. To one side sat Vossenack's translator, a thin young State Department aide who had graduated from the Vietnamese language course at the Army Language School in Monterey with honors.

"It is most courteous of you to ask us to attend. We will happily convey your request to President Diem, but I am in a position to say that he will . . . most . . . definitely—assuredly be happy with the arrangements," said the translator.

Vossenack smiled. "Perhaps you will also do me the personal favor, General Dang, of conveying to the president my hopes for a meeting within the next few days to discuss several issues of mutual interest to our two nations. One topic I would like to discuss is the matter of land reform. My government is very concerned that present progress in this area seems to be very much behind schedule."

The two generals still smiled, but Vossenack could tell that now they were watching him carefully. Dang, the one in the white suit, was chief of the president's cabinet, a position that gave him a lot of influence in the government. He was also the general who let his division get chewed up by the Vietcong down in the Delta back in January. Dang, in fact, was not even with his division at the time, preferring instead the easy life and political intrigues in Saigon. The other general, what was his name? Ba, he was, well, there were stories about his black-market connections. According to a CIA report, some of his officers were selling stuff to the Vietcong. Vossenack sighed inwardly. A hell of a bunch to work with.

"I would also like to discuss with the president the current problems with the Buddhists. I know this has been a recurring problem, and you have discussed it many times with my predecessor, Ambassador Simpson. Frankly, gentlemen, it confuses the American people when they see these demonstrations on television. And it gives some of our congressmen, unfortunately perhaps, doubts about the wisdom of continuing the present high level of aid that we provide your country. As I said to President Diem when I presented my credentials—and I'm sure this has been discussed with my predecessor—the United States would look very favorably on a compromise with the Buddhist leadership for the duration of this present crisis. I strongly urge President Diem that this be done at the earliest opportunity."

Vossenack paused while the translation took place. The two generals nodded and smiled. Both spoke some basic English, but it was easier to use a translator for more involved ideas.

"In addition, gentlemen," Vossenack pressed on, "we must come to some agreement about the present use of your Special Forces troops as a political unit rather than as a combat one. Again, many in the United States are having doubts about our financial support of these troops. Many feel, both in the military and in the Congress, that the Special Forces should be assigned to field duties rather than being used in these raids on Buddhist temples." Vossenack stopped, watching for some acknowledgment from the two Vietnamese generals.

Dang began to speak, his broad face beaming. "We are in sincere agreement that certain changes should take place. But there are difficulties in implementing a correct program, or in what we—in what we can do, with the present terrorist situation in progress. Perhaps there will be ways in the future." Sorenson, the young State Department translator, glanced at Vossenack, but the ambassador was sitting back on the sofa, his legs carefully crossed, smiling politely. Dang went on, his smile broader.

"As regards to a meeting between you, Mr. Ambassador, and the president. It is difficult because of the president's schedule. He devotes himself to the people. He is constantly traveling. Opening schools and hospitals. Even supervising the education of teachers. I am sure, however, that a—a meeting can be . . . scheduled—arranged, in the very near future." Sorenson's voice droned to a stop.

Vossenack nodded as if agreeing with what the general had said. Shit. He hadn't been able to get in to see Diem for days now. Washington was on his ass. Kennedy, Rusk, McNamara—they all wanted results. The National Security Council was divided. There was an election coming up. The U.S. had sixteen thousand men in this goddamn little country, and he couldn't even get to see its president.

There was a tap on the door, and Hong, the ambassador's servant, padded in quietly with more coffee on a silver tray. As he quietly refilled the cups on a low table, Dang spoke slowly in English.

"I understand this village not far from Saigon."

"No, not far. Ben Thong, about twenty-four kilometers northeast. As you know, my wife has taken a personal interest in the hamlet. I'm sure she will also be delighted if the president can attend the official opening."

"President Diem find these occasion he very much like."

"Will you also be able to attend, General Dang?"

"I have regret, no. On November third, I have official—ah, duty—duty?"—he looked at the interpreter—"to attend. There are so many demand on time."

The three men nodded and smiled.

Lazar read the message again carefully. The runner squatted on the floor, his face and body soaked with sweat. Lazar read it a third time, studying it for every nuance, every last iota of information. He felt a surge of excitement. An idea, a gleam of light that could evolve into possibilities that could stagger the mind. For a moment he was stunned with its brilliance. It was the perfect way to accomplish the mission. He stood up and walked to the map on the wall of his bunker. Then he turned and smiled at the runner, nodding. The man quickly left. Lazar turned back to the map, tracing out a route with his finger tip. He'd need to know more, of course, much more. Security arrangements, number of people, routes. Yes, his excitement mounted. Why not? As he touched the map, he noticed his hand was shaking, his pulse rapid. For a fleeting moment, he wondered if his grandfather would be proud of him.

7

MARGARET VOSSENACK WAS sitting naked in her dressing room. The steam from her shower was clearing. The exhaust fan seldom seemed to work, no matter what was done to it. She looked at her reflection in the vanity mirror closely as she brushed her hair. Her age was beginning to show, she decided, the streaks of gray in her hair, a steady thickening around the waist. Perhaps when Robert—she always referred to her husband as Robert—was reassigned, and they returned to the States, she would go to one of those resorts where they pampered you and somehow worked a sort of sorcery of rejuvenation, spiriting away the years with massages and carrot juice.

Robert. Through the open door of her dressing room she could see into the bedroom, where her maid was laying out her clothes. Margaret looked at herself again in the mirror. Her body was white but for the tan on her legs and arms, the result of tennis games twice a week. But even the exercise did not compensate for the passing years: She knew the vitality of youth had long since vanished. She touched herself carefully. Her body was still good, still firm, not slack and wasted. If only Robert could . . .

She had been married to her husband for twenty-two years, and he was thirteen years her senior. Her father had been an executive with General Motors and a dollar-a-year man with the Roosevelt Administration. Robert had been an army captain, steadily working himself upwards, already noticed as a smart, ambitious officer, and she had met him at a party when she was a pretty twenty-year-old. It had not been easy to overlook the difference in the ages and their backgrounds: her family had misgivings. Robert, after all, while an officer and a gentleman, had come from, well, a more humble background. There had been talk—Grosse Pointe gossip—that she was marrying a little beneath her station.

But Robert had earned his promotions. He had done it all himself. "I don't have the advantages they have," he would say. "I have to work for whatever I can get in life." It was unspoken who "they" were, but "they" were the people with background and wealth, who went to the good schools and got the good positions—like the daughter of a General Motors executive.

Why, where, did they lose something? The higher Robert rose, the more polished he became, the more prestigious the positions, so the more distant became their relationship, the more ordered their existences, until it seemed to merge into a seamless blend, an official round of cocktail parties, receptions, quiet good manners. She was expected to be a gracious hostess, to look like a general's wife, to make polite talk, the questions to be just right—not pointed or difficult. And she did her job well, even excelled at it. It was, after all, something she had been trained to do. But there was a lack, she hesitated to define it—what?—a sense of . . . touching. They had one son, Robert, Jr., now a cadet at West Point. A handsome young man. A son to be proud of. The last time he was home, he had lectured her on the failure of American policy in postwar Germany. He had not realized, had not even sought to find out, that she had known as much about the problems of a divided Germany as he did.

The maid tapped on the door of the bathroom.

"Clothes ready, *Madame*."

Margaret slipped on a bathrobe. She touched the things on her dressing table, the personal things she liked and touched every day. A shell-backed mirror, a present from her sister, now married to a group vice-president with Chase Manhattan. Her silver brushes. She glimpsed herself again in the vanity mirror. She led a good life. Any woman would be proud of a husband like Robert. A lieutenant general. An ambassador. She looked at his photograph standing on the vanity. The slate gray eyes beneath the braid-encrusted peak of his cap, the grim mouth, his jaw rigid and set. It was so much like him. When was the last time he had really laughed? Not the hearty, booming, locker-room laugh of the senior military officers and business executives they seemed to mimic, but just—laugh. She touched the frame of his picture. I must get one of him in civilian clothes, she thought absently.

Their conversations were stilted these days, little beyond small talk. At breakfast that morning, she had tried to talk to him about his work, about the political situation in Vietnam and the increased confrontations between the government and the Buddhist monks.

"The government will solve its problems with the Buddhists," he said irritably. It was the end of the discussion.

She felt hurt and resentful. For an instant she wanted to say something sharply.

Vossenack had wiped his mouth with his napkin and stood up.

"Start dinner without me, dear. Sorry. I'll eat at the MACV officers' club today. I'm meeting most of the afternoon with General Bachelor and his staff."

She pushed her thoughts aside.

"Oh, I had a letter from Jane today. Bill's been accepted by Yale Law."

"Oh, great," he said. "Always knew that boy would

go far." He checked through some documents in his briefcase. The ambassador's chauffeur, a stout Vietnamese, appeared in the doorway to their breakfast room, his cap in his hand.

"Must go, dear," Vossenack aimed a kiss at her cheek. "Give your sister my congratulations, will you." He hurried out.

She sighed now, looking at his photograph. Perhaps her work with the settlement at Ben Thong would be something of importance to her husband. It was his idea to ask Diem to attend the dedication ceremonies. Keeping busy was the answer. After all, it was expected of her position.

"Run," Sanders roared, "run, you shitheads."

The three sweating, dirt-encrusted men raced past the sandbagged enclosure. There was a tremendous crack and a shower of dirt, sand and canvas shot into the air. Chu staggered, bumping into McWaters, and both fell splashing into the mud. Le wavered to a stop, his chest heaving.

Sanders strolled over. He was naked to the waist, wearing only a pair of cut-off khaki shorts. The sparse black hair on his chest glistened with sweat. There were streaks of mud on his legs. He held a small detonating device in his hand. He shook his head.

"Nope. Not good enough, are we? Too much soft living, that's the trouble."

McWaters lay on the ground, chest heaving.

"Sir," he gasped, "why is this necessary?"

"Because, Lieutenant McWaters, when we go looking for the VC, we'll be out there on our own. We'll no longer be in our game. We'll be in theirs. But mainly it's necessary because I say so. Now, let's do it again and this time put some effort into it."

Le chattered wearily to Chu, and Sanders suddenly whirled and kicked him hard.

"Git." A deep snarl. The three men staggered off.

They were in a coastal province north of Saigon. A lush, heavily farmed region where bright green mountains rose from plains that were divided into the squares and rectangles of ricefields with almost mathematical precision. Sanders had found an old abandoned bunker, little more than several layers of sandbags stacked atop boards set on a few dirt-filled fifty-five-gallon oil drums. The drums were pitted with rust, while the bags were rotting, dribbling dirt into the muddy ground. He looked at the bunker with satisfaction. Not far from Saigon, it was reputed to be secure country. Nearby was a river and, about a half mile away, a small village, one of those new strategic hamlets that some called "agrovilles," one-story huts with tile roofs and a few miserable garden plots surrounded by a fence made of interwoven strands of barbed wire. This village was better constructed than most.

The next day a truck had delivered food, medical supplies, extra pairs of fatigues, and weapons—a box of grenades and an assortment of well-worn .30-caliber carbines and .45-caliber "grease guns." Sanders had kicked the fatigues aside, looked at the dirty weapons with disgust, and put everyone to work cleaning and oiling them.

Since then, for five days now, they had been training from before dawn to long after dark. There was constant running, crawling through mud, finding their way—splashing across paddy fields in the darkness—by compass and map. Sanders taught them how to set and prime a demolition charge. How to camouflage a booby trap. How to crawl across a field and leave nothing to show you've been there. They had eaten nothing but one ball of rice each day and a canteen of water—except for a snake that McWaters had eaten and then thrown up. Sanders barked and hounded them constantly. At one point, when Chu was slow in getting up, he had pulled the Vietnamese to his feet and then knocked him down again with a savage back-handed blow. Strangely, the two Vietnamese seemed to enjoy the exercise and now chattered together as if they had been friends all their lives. To McWaters, however, it was a kind of nightmare. By the third night he was dreaming of pancakes flooded with maple syrup, giant hamburgers, and tall glasses of cold milk. To say the least, this was not what he expected when he decided to take Naval ROTC at Princeton.

On the evening of the fifth day, Sanders had relented somewhat and allowed them to prepare a decent meal. Le had cooked them *pho*, a sort of Vietnamese soup made of beef and noodles. Now they sat outside the bunker in the moist twilight, the two Vietnamese still happily spooning rice into their mouths as they chatted, while Sanders, comfortably smoking, and McWaters sat back against the sandbags.

"What are you doin' here, Lieutenant?" The same harsh voice, but McWaters had noticed Sanders had drunk nothing since he had arrived in Vietnam. Their relationship had not improved since the States. It was formal and stiff, both addressing each other by their military rank. It was an unspoken barrier between them that McWaters's prime function on the mission was to keep tabs on Sanders and report back immediately to Vossenack if the major so much as looked the wrong way.

"You're never going to believe this," said McWaters, aching, filthy, and so tired he could hardly keep awake. "I thought my life was too comfortable. Really. It was the Peace Corps or the navy." He managed to smile ruefully.

"I believe it," grunted Sanders.

McWaters told Sanders about his family's large Tudor house in Westchester. His father's furniture manufacturing company. Their vacations in Jamaica and Aspen. His prep school in Connecticut. "I wanted to see some military service. The navy seemed right. I didn't want to get stuck on a ship so I got myself assigned to the CIA. I plan to go on to law school when I get out. Then I want to go into politics. A military record can't hurt." He stopped lamely, embarrassed somehow. Sitting on the ground outside a collapsing bunker in Vietnam, training every day to kill in every way imaginable seemed to make his ambitions trivial, even petty.

Sanders had said nothing, merely looked at the lieutenant, and McWaters couldn't be sure if he was smiling or not. Suddenly McWaters realized that, right now, what he really wanted to do in life was to earn the esteem of Sanders. The feeling left him puzzled, disconcerted.

"What do you think will happen here, Major? I mean this Communist insurgency is going to get beaten, isn't it?"

Sanders studied the young man.

"I don't think too hard about the politics, Lieutenant, but I would say it's really difficult to tell at this point. A guerrilla war is hard to fight militarily. We made some headway against the Japanese in World War Two doing this sort of thing, but not much, frankly. The British did it in Malaya, but they were able to isolate the Communist guerrillas from the population. The situation here is not really the same, but it could be fought pretty much the same way. Maybe with the help of some American technology. But I have my doubts whether this Diem government can do it. Diem and his family," Sanders shook his head, "I don't know." He took a drag on his cigarette and coughed hard, holding his arm over his face. "I think there're two ways we can go at this point," he went on. "Either we throw everything we have at the VC. Right now. A couple of divisions. Bombers. The works. Really swamp 'em. Or else we do it their way. Fight them on their own terms. Root 'em out one at a time with small, guerrilla-type operations. Go for the infrastructure. Every dirty trick we can. But that will take years. The first option is politically unpopular. The second, well, that'll be unpopular, too. Americans are not a patient people. Anyway, the decisions will be made in Washington, not here."

"But how can you take on a mission like this if you have doubts about whether we can win or not?"

Sanders smiled.

"Well, for one thing, Lieutenant, it's a job that I can do better than most people. I'm good at it. And that's all I do. I don't have to make the big decisions. That's for those assholes in Washington who think they know what they're doin'. For another, well, nothing says we have to lose. If we handle it right, we'll win. Besides, I think it's more their war," he gestured towards Chu and Le, "than ours. How much are they willing to fight against the Reds? It's their country. And so far, they haven't shown me they're motivated to put out the effort."

"But what about the U.S.? It's surely not in our interest for Southeast Asia to go Communist. And it will without our help."

"Possibly. Maybe we do need to do more than what we've been doing so far. We stopped the Reds in Korea and at least saved half a country. But half a country here. Half there. It's hard to see Americans die for something like that." He shrugged.

"So what do you suggest we do?"

"For one thing we can work smarter, not harder. I was at a lecture on the South Vietnamese Army at MACV a couple of days ago. I'd say we took a wrong turn back in 1959. Apparently, back when the South Vietnamese National Army was formed, it had a number of Light

Divisions, units light on artillery and armor and heavy transport. The idea was that they could go into the country and fight guerrillas and not be tied to a lot of logistical support. Seems a good idea to me. Well, MAAG, as it was known then, got a hair up its ass with the notion that the South Vietnamese Army should really be like the American Army, with heavy divisions so it could take on North Vietnam in a conventional war. So, they reorganized the Light Divisions out of existence. They beefed them up with a lot of artillery and heavy mortars, just like an American unit equipped to fight in Europe. MAAG said the South Vietnamese could still go into the jungle, only the artillery needed transportation. But what happened in real, actual life was that the South Vietnamese commanders became unwilling to move beyond the range of their artillery. So, in effect, the ARVN became roadbound. The Reds had a field day in the villages out in the boonies. And we lost the initiative." Sanders flipped away his cigarette butt. "Still, what do I know? As our ambassador would say, I'm 'just a civilian.' "

They lapsed into silence. Le was scratching at his testicles, telling Chu a lewd story. A sliver of moon dropped a soft silver polish on the distant rice paddies. Trees etched themselves black against a lighter sky. From the hamlet, a dog barked and then was silent. Night insects droned. For a moment McWaters felt oddly relaxed, the contentment that comes from a day of hard work. Sanders suddenly stood up and kicked sandy dirt over their low fire.

"Let's go. We've got a map exercise to do, and this time it's going to get serious." He grinned as he saw them scurry around. "Come on, you bastards. You've been eating too good. Tonight we're going to catch ourselves some nice big frogs to eat." And he laughed hugely. The three other men wearily followed his laughter as it disappeared into the night.

Deep within the palace, the mandarin watched the police colonel make his report. The colonel was sweating in the heat of the small room. The room was windowless and the mandarin had not left it all day. His watch said twelve. It was midnight, he realized.

"Are you sure that is the target?"

The police colonel squirmed. He owed his job, his life to the mandarin. How many papers in this room, he wondered, in the stuffed drawers in the desk, in the stacked chests, had his name on them? The mandarin, sitting on the brocaded couch, dressed in black, with black eyes that seemed to see into his soul, a smile on the thin purple lips, did he know about the colonel's wife and her black-market deals? About his illegal currency transactions? Sweat poured down the colonel's round face as he thought of his contacts with a certain merchant in Cholon who was said to have links with the Liberation Front.

He said, "It's hard to say at present, Excellency. The suspect died during the interrogation, but he tried to save his life with a scrap of information. I am certain that the Communists are planning something big. It's my guess, from the information I can put together, that this is the target."

"Again, how did the, ah, suspect know this?" The purple lips seemed hardly to move.

"His brother is with the Communist terrorists in a camp somewhere west of Ben Suc. A few days ago a courier came to the camp with information from Saigon. The courier was young and very talkative. There also appears to be some, ah, resentment between the NLF and the cadre from the North." The colonel paused uncertainly. The mandarin's family was from North Vietnam.

The mandarin seemed to gaze at something behind the colonel's head. The policeman fidgeted, wondering how soon he could get out into the air. He felt as though he was suffocating.

"Keep trying. Now the other thing. What else have you found out?"

The colonel's heart beat wildly.

"More rumors, Excellency. Talk here and there. Nothing much to go on."

"You say General Ba is involved?"

"Yes, Excellency, and,"—the colonel gasped as if finding it hard to breathe—"it also appears General Dang might be implicated—although, again," hastily, "I don't have definite information." The colonel was trembling now. There was a burst of loud American jazz abruptly cut off by a slammed door. Which one of Nhu's daughters was that? Perhaps it was his wife, the Madame herself. No. Impossible. She was out of the country. The colonel squirmed uncomfortably, his necktie seemed to be choking him.

"General Dang." The mandarin said it softly, with a smile. The tips of his fingers touched. "You are most dependable, Colonel. I am very grateful. You will, of course, keep this information to yourself."

"Of course, Excellency."

"You may be sure that your advancement in the nation's service will be looked upon favorably by my brother, the president."

The policeman beamed.

The mandarin reached for a small booklet.

"Allow me to present to you my latest work. It describes my philosophy toward land reform. A very misrepresented concept."

The colonel took the material with a show of eagerness.

"I will read it with great care, Excellency." He knew he would be able to understand barely a word of it. Few people in Vietnam could understand the mandarin's idea on how the country should be run, a strange philosophy that rejected both capitalism and socialism.

When the colonel had left, leaving behind a sour odor of sweat and eau d'cologne, the mandarin sat thinking, a thin smile on his dark, handsome face. An ornate box sat on his desk. A pipe, he deserved one. He kneaded the ball of opium into the tiny copper bowl. The colonel had brought some astounding news, but it was not time yet to divulge it to his brother. No, his brother was too impulsive. He would wait for the best opportunity. If they timed it right, they could catch everyone—every single traitor. He sucked in deeply. He had plenty of time, all the time in the world.

8

THE AMBASSADOR'S WIFE sat in the back of the air-conditioned Cadillac watching the geometry of the paddy fields drift past the tinted window. Occasionally, her chauffeur pulled over to the side of the narrow highway to let a convoy of army trucks move slowly past in a cloud of red dust. There were signs of the military everywhere. MPs stood guard at crossroads while a flight of three American helicopters beat their way overhead. Yet Margaret felt no fear. This was a secure area, well controlled by the government. Two jeeps, four American MPs in each, followed closely behind her Cadillac.

The big black automobile, which drew stares from the Vietnamese they passed, swung off the asphalt highway onto a dirt-and-gravel road signposted for Ben Thong. On her right, through the trees, she could see a river and beyond the river more paddy fields. In the distance green mountains rose perhaps seven or eight hundred meters. A farmer in a conical hat was plowing his swampy field with a water buffalo. It was picturesque, like a postcard of Vietnam. Wish you were here, she thought. The war seemed distant and remote.

She had taken a personal interest in Ben Thong almost from the time they had arrived in Vietnam. She had wanted to do something, involve herself in some project to directly help the Vietnamese. Robert had agreed. It would look good for the embassy, he had said. She had made discreet inquiries. The Canadian ambassador's wife had told her about Ben Thong. When Margaret first saw the hamlet it was no more than a few thatched shacks within a bamboo enclosure. Barely fifty people lived there, no school, many of the children suffering from God knows what diseases, the adults listless, with the pathetic helplessness of refugees. And they *were* refugees. The government had bulldozed their old village, claiming it was too close to a Vietcong-controlled area, and moved the entire population in closer to Saigon.

But it was embassy funds, American funds, that had paid for the construction of better housing, a two-room school, even a small clinic with a nurse. Other families had been moved in. Now the hamlet's population was two hundred. In a few weeks, there would be a formal dedication, a recognition of the work done by the United States in helping Vietnam. Robert would be there, and so would President Diem. It made Margaret feel proud of how much she had contributed.

The Vietnamese village officials—the mayor, his assistant, and the security chief—were courteous and solicitous. With the nurse acting as interpreter, they walked around the hamlet in the humid heat, discussing the details of the forthcoming dedication ceremony. Small children stared at them, their mothers smiling. Margaret glanced down at her white shoes, now covered with a film of red dust. Like parts of the Midwest, she thought. The village was looking a lot better. I must get more paint for the school. And perhaps some pictures for the walls. She felt content in Ben Thong, out of sight of the MPs who remained lounging around the jeeps. She felt truly by herself, handling something she alone had created.

They strolled along a gravel path. Something must be done about the vegetable plots, they're looking quite bedraggled. "The vegetable gardens. Ask them to do something about the vegetable gardens," she said to the young nurse, a smiling girl in a snow white uniform.

A long conversation in Vietnamese followed, with the three Vietnamese nodding and smiling.

"Perhaps we can have some flowers along the paths," said the ambassador's wife. She kneaded a handkerchief in the palm of her hand, trying to soak up the perspiration.

The three Vietnamese men looked puzzled.

"Flowers," said Margaret. "Oh dear. Bright." She gestured vaguely. The nurse was chattering in Vietnamese, while the men looked blankly at her.

Suddenly there was a terrific explosion beyond the village. She saw a mass of dirt and mud fly into the air, and a great cloud of bluish smoke sailed above the treetops. The detonation shook the buildings, the windows rattling in their frames.

"What on earth . . . ?" Margaret stared dumbfounded, but the Vietnamese seemed unconcerned.

"What was that?"

"Oh, that American man," said the nurse, smiling. "His name San-der'. He give, ah, candy to children."

Feet pounded on the path and four towering MPs came running around the corner of a building, red faced, rifles ready.

"Are you all right, ma'am?" said the sergeant anxiously. He had visions of the ambassador's wife being hurt and his being busted to private on the spot.

"I'm fine, sergeant. It's quite all right, I can handle it."

"Are you sure, ma'am? We were told this is a secure area, but—"

"Yes, sergeant. I'll take full responsibility. Everything is fine. I'll be back to the car shortly."

The four MPs reluctantly retreated, the sergeant looking worried.

"I can't allow this. Where is this Sanders? I'll have a

word with him," said Margaret. She was angry. How dare he disrupt her village.

The nurse pointed out the path to take. It went through a grove of tall elephant grass and bushes, following the river. Margaret walked along by herself. The dirt path seemed to wind around, almost doubling back on itself. It was quite pleasant here. Insects hummed in the silence. A gentle breeze bent the tall grass. Here and there through the grass and the bushes she could see the flash of sunlight on the river.

Suddenly a man, almost naked, ran across the path ahead of her. She stopped, not sure if she should call out. There was silence. The insects droned on. She had only caught a glimpse of the man but she thought it had looked like that young Lieutenant McWaters she had been introduced to at an embassy reception last week. How strange. Margaret walked on. For a moment she thought she saw an ugly face leering at her from the bushes, but when she looked again, it was gone. It must have been her imagination.

The second explosion also took her by surprise. On the other side of the bushes, there was a bang that almost deafened her, and a great gout of water and reddish mud sailed into the air. She leaped frantically sideways but, too late, much of it soaked her.

Margaret stood speechless with rage, staring at her wet dress streaked with brown and red, her hair plastered to one side of her face.

"Damn," she screamed.

Angrily, she stormed through the bushes.

For a moment she couldn't see anything except a great patch of mud spreading across the surface of the river in widening ripples. Then she saw the naked back of a man standing in the water. He was picking up dead fish floating on the surface.

"Mr. Sanders? Mr. Sanders you must stop this immediately," she called, almost spluttering with rage. "You can't do this."

The man in the river casually picked up a fish floating belly up and turned around slowly. With a start she saw it was the man who Robert had introduced as Major Sanders.

"What's the trouble, ma'am?" He seemed amused when he saw her condition, and this enraged her still further.

"This is absolutely intolerable. You're disrupting the entire hamlet, and—and look what you've done to me." Her ears still rang from the explosion. Tears came into her eyes. She pulled a gob of mud out of her hair fiercely and flung it down. The ambassador's wife was suddenly conscious of the man's nakedness. The water running down his massive chest. The graying hair plastered across his forehead. The serene eyes, a startling blue, that regarded her from a huge, crudely shaped face.

"You're Mrs. Vossenack, aren't you?"

"Er—yes, I am. And this village," she gestured behind her, trying to hold up her hair with the other hand, "is a very special place. It has just been built to settle . . ."—she almost said refugees—"relocated Vietnamese, and there's an official dedication ceremony here in a few weeks. President Diem will attend, and it's very important for the United States Embassy and our work here. So you see . . . ," her voice began to trail away. Sanders was coming toward her. He was coming out of the water with an armful of dead fish. He was stark naked. "Really, Major Sanders." She almost giggled. And then she saw the massive scar deep across his chest.

He grinned at her. "I wasn't expecting company, and I forgot to pack my swimsuit, anyway." He picked up a pair of dirty shorts from the bank and pulled them on unselfconsciously. "Perhaps this will help." He tossed a green tee-shirt toward her.

"What on earth are you doing here?—or perhaps I'm not supposed to ask." She felt her anger evaporating.

He grinned again. His face almost looked pleasant when he smiled. "Ask me no questions, I'll tell you no lies. Anyway, I can say the same about you."

She sat down on the bank beside him, kicking off her soaked shoes—one of the heels had somehow broken off—and trying to wipe the mud off her dress and legs.

"I'm helping to develop the hamlet. Organizing things. Getting the school going. It's important, you know. For us to help these people." She looked quickly at him to see if he would laugh. But Sanders merely looked back at her steadily. "I hope you don't think this sort of thing is a waste of time."

"No, I wouldn't think so."

"But you don't think it's much use," she persisted.

"Well, do you think we can do that much, Mrs. Vossenack? Vietnam has been here a long time."

"But don't you see, it's still back almost in the Dark Ages. There's so much that could be done here. Even in agriculture—" she stopped. Sanders was picking mud from between his toes.

"I suppose you think the right answer is the military way." She almost continued, "like my husband."

"It's one answer."

"If we're here we should do something to help them. Something more than just protecting them from terrorists in black pajamas. We have so much and they have so little." She picked at some drying mud on her face.

"Perhaps they have more than you give them credit for."

"Yes," she said abruptly, "fifty-seven varieties of diseases."

"Here, you've missed some." He took the tee-shirt out of her hand and, with surprising gentleness, wiped some mud from her hair.

81

"I must look a sight." She began to giggle again, and then they were both laughing.

"What kind of a soldier are you, Major Sanders? You don't look, if I may say so, like the usual professional American military man."

"I'm strictly an amateur, lady. I just get paid for what I do."

"Oh, I see." She instantly regretted the way she had said it.

Sanders looked at her, his serene blue eyes untroubled and clear. He had finished digging the mud from his toes and was now rubbing it off his legs and arms.

"Don't judge me too harshly." She was surprised when he began to recite a poem:

> "These, in the day when heaven is falling,
>   The hour when earth's foundations fled,
> Followed their mercenary calling
>   And took their wages and are dead."

"Oh, I've heard that before," said Margaret. "Housman. How does the rest of it go?"

> "Their shoulders held the sky suspended;
>   They stood, and earth's foundations stay;
> What God abandoned, these defended,
>   And saved the sum of things for pay."

"Are you defending what God has abandoned?"

"Hell, lady, someone has to."

They laughed. And then both fell silent. The sky was clouding to the southwest, wind blowing in from the China Sea. Another rainstorm on the way. Margaret handed back the dirty tee-shirt.

"I must be getting back. The MPs will come looking for me soon."

They stood up. Sanders pulled on the tee-shirt, seemingly oblivious to its stains and dirt. She noticed he was the same height as her but looked shorter because of his husky build and massive shoulders.

"Good-bye, Major Sanders. Perhaps . . . ," she looked amused, "I was going to say 'perhaps we'll see more of each other' but that's hardly likely on my part. Anyway, perhaps we'll see each other again." She held out her hand. It became lost in his huge paw. She was the gracious ambassador's wife again. He looked at her steadily for a moment.

"You never know, Mrs. Vossenack."

As she walked away along the dirt path, she felt him watching her. And without looking back she had the strange feeling that he belonged here, to the dirt pathway, the paddy fields and the river shining in the sun. As if this was his land and he was more at home here than she, or Robert, could ever be.

The MPs gaped at her when she walked out to the shiny Cadillac, swinging her shoes in one hand.

"We can go now, sergeant," she called, and jumped nimbly into the car.

On her way back to Saigon, the limousine splashing along the wet road, she smiled when she thought of what Robert's expression would be when he saw her. And for a moment, she also allowed herself to think of the hulking form of Major Sanders.

9

How much longer? McWaters staggered, sweat spraying from his hair.

All day they had been marching without food or water. His fatigue shirt was black with the sweat that streamed down his face and arms. A cloud of biting insects buzzed around his head. The straps on his pack cut into his shoulders, and his carbine seemed to have added another ten pounds. About twenty yards ahead Sanders walked along steadily, never seeming to vary his pace or pause in the rhythm of his march. Straggling behind McWaters were Chu and Le, padding along with only an occasional grunt of effort.

They had been moving for two days. Away from the heavily populated coastal plain with its rice paddies, orchards, and irrigation canals. The open country was giving way to thin stands of timber and gradually thickening underbrush and bamboo thickets. Whenever they came to a break in the trees, McWaters could see mountains in the distance. The trail was hard-packed with a tangle of brush on either side. In places, the trees met overhead. Around midday they had been soaked by a brief shower, and the trees still dripped, the drops hitting the skin with a snap that almost left a welt. They skirted a large rubber plantation, its trees planted in neat rows, but it looked abandoned.

Sanders had let them eat at the end of their first day and then given them a few hours of sleep. McWaters had wrapped himself in his blanket, shivering from the sudden cold. It must have been about forty degrees when he woke up. It was still dark. They had rolled up their blankets, hoisted their packs onto aching shoulders, and started out again. When McWaters had asked Sanders where they were going, Sanders would only say cryptically, "We're going to let Lazar find us."

They were heading in a northeasterly direction, but at times they seemed to wander to the north and west. Sanders would stop occasionally and look at a map and consult with Le about the area. The Vietnamese would wave his arms about energetically and grin broadly, but whether he made any sense to Sanders, McWaters could not tell. It was if Sanders had some general idea of where to go, but he was really waiting for someone, for permission to approach.

Sanders seemed to be moving carefully, inspecting the trail, as they marched. His head and eyes were constantly moving, and often he stopped to inspect a clump of bushes or tree branches that came low over the trail before proceeding. But they saw nothing, no sign of the Vietcong.

They stopped when it grew dark, camping near a stream that flowed through a small hollow, forming a shiny pool. But it was deceptive. The water covered rotting vegetation festering in slime. Small bubbles of poisonous gas broke on the surface. There was a sudden rustle in the grass, and McWaters bounded to his feet in time to see the tail of a bright red snake slither away.

"Did you see that?" he gasped. He had a loathing fear of snakes.

"It's gone now," said Sanders nonchalantly. "Be glad it didn't bite you on the pecker. You'd have had to do some quick thinking."

Trembling with exhaustion, McWaters sat down and spooned corned beef and cheese into his mouth from the K-ration can, clutching it to his chest. Even Le was silent. Both Vietnamese prepared their own meals and were eating what looked like dried prunes and rice.

Saying little to each other, the team rolled in ground sheets and blankets and went to sleep. Something woke McWaters before dawn. The jungle seemed to be moaning from the wind. Another rainstorm on the way. The dark sky was without stars. He heard another sound, strangely out of place, and then he realized it was Sanders singing somewhere. McWaters couldn't make out the song, but it sounded almost like a hymn. Stiffly, shivering with the cold, he began to pack away his ground sheet and blanket. The singing had stopped, although Sanders was nowhere to be seen. Chu and Le were moving silently around. Suddenly a muffled roar sounded in the distance. The two Vietnamese stood absolutely still, staring off into the woods, the trees no more than vague shapes. Sanders casually walked into the camp, as if on a Sunday stroll. He nodded pleasantly to McWaters.

"Tiger somewhere."

McWaters knew that there were tigers in Vietnam but he imagined somehow they were only found in thick rain forest and jungle. The idea that one was nearby seemed preposterous.

"Do you think it will come any closer?"

"No, it's going away—hear that?" Another roar, more distant this time.

"Are there a lot around here?"

"Not too many probably. It's unusual for one to be so close to civilization. But there are tigers in these hills, and wild boars, barking deer, and something called a clouded leopard."

"A clouded leopard?" The name was fascinating.

The husky major was already swinging his pack onto his shoulders. "It has a dark, grayish kind of coat. It's really a species of tiger. Something you wouldn't want to meet alone. The Vietnamese think it's a special kind of animal, and they have all sorts of legends about it. They think it's like a spirit of a dead person or a phantom in the jungle. That sort of thing. Let's go."

The day became a repetition of the two before. They were now moving through heavy forest with thickets of underbrush and scrub. Here and there were dense groves of bamboo, and the country was becoming more broken. There was a sudden crash in the bushes and several roebuck bounded away. The two Vietnamese laughed and pointed, Chu making a shooting sound.

A torrential rain left them soaked and then steam lifted lazily from the wet earth with the heat of midday. To the southwest the sky was leaden but by the afternoon it cleared. McWaters called out a remark about the height of the bamboo, some of it twenty or thirty feet high.

"That's female bamboo," said Sanders. "The little stuff is the male."

McWaters noticed that Sanders was not moving as easily now. The stocky man's breathing was labored, rasping, and the back of his shirt was soaked with sweat. The lieutenant wondered if the old chest wound was bothering him.

Toward the evening they stopped and made camp. As McWaters looked around he suddenly realized that he was seeing things he had seen that morning.

"We've come in a circle," he exploded. "What the hell's going on?" He was baffled and angry. The lieutenant stood up and faced Sanders, who was eating unconcernedly.

"Correct," said Sanders, forking in a mouthful of beans.

"What's the idea?" Almost a shout.

The two Vietnamese sat silently, watching. It occurred to McWaters that they had probably realized long ago what was happening but had said nothing.

"Because," said Sanders, leaning back on his pack, "we don't have anywhere to go just yet." His face looked haggard, and McWaters realized that the march had been hard on him.

McWaters sat down, the strength suddenly gone from his legs. He realized how tired and worn out he was.

"Why," he said with an almost physical effort, "didn't we just get ourselves flown out here on a Huey?"

Sanders laid back with his hands behind his head, eyes half closed.

"Because," he said again, "they wouldn't be able to see us and get word back to Lazar. What's more, we would have risked the Huey. Somebody may have got killed just because we didn't want to walk in."

"I still don't—" McWaters stopped when Sanders suddenly motioned at him. All four men instantly picked up their weapons. They were camped to one side of a small clearing that opened up from the trail. Heavy vegetation surrounded them—trees, bushes, bamboo. McWaters was suddenly aware of the silence. Sanders motioned again, and the two Vietnamese rolled away, their weapons ready. The navy lieutenant pulled back the bolt on his carbine and let it go forward gently, but Sanders raised a cautious hand.

"Don't fire until I say so," he whispered.

The clearing, about thirty yards across, was bathed in bright sunshine but streaked with lengthening shadows, and McWaters tried to see into the deep shade beneath the trees on the other side, but there was no movement, nothing.

Still they lay there not moving. The minutes ticked away. An unseen animal chattered uneasily. McWaters's mouth was dry and he had a wrenching feeling in his gut like it was suddenly empty. He realized he was afraid. There was death nearby. Perhaps all around them. The seconds of his life were dribbling out into the steamy air.

He was about to stage whisper something to Sanders when he saw a movement on the other side of the clearing. He raised his carbine, but a firm hand came down on the barrel. Sanders shook his head.

McWaters blinked and then he realized a man had stepped out of the shadows. He stood at the very edge of the shade, appearing as a darker patch so that you had to look hard to see him. A Vietnamese wearing black pajamas and a floppy hat, a black-and-white checkered scarf around his neck. And McWaters realized that this was the first enemy soldier he had seen. A small man carrying a short rifle slung across his back.

"San-der'." The call was high-pitched, almost unintelligible. "San-der'." The VC was waving, motioning them to come forward.

"Stay here," said Sanders softly. "If anything happens get out of here." He motioned to Chu and both stood up and walked out into the bright sunlight. They walked across the clearing, Sanders strolling, Chu loping along beside him. If the VC opened fire they would both be dead in seconds. McWaters saw them walk up to the enemy soldier and start talking. The Vietnamese was gesturing. Sanders seemed to be asking Chu something. They talked on. McWaters glanced over at Le. The Vietnamese was crouched behind a bush, his .45 "grease gun" ready. Sweat beaded his face. McWaters knew that Le would be shot immediately if the VC captured him. A cloud drifted across the sun, and it was suddenly darker. The three men continued to talk, and then abruptly Sanders and Chu walked back. The VC disappeared into the shadows again.

Sanders dropped his pack and carbine on the ground.

"Lazar wants to talk. I'm going with the VC. I want you and Chu and Le to stay here. They won't do anything to you. I want you to stay here for twenty-four hours. And then if I don't show get going. As fast as you can."

"I don't like it. Lazar is going to kill you. Let's get out of here. Come back with a battalion of ARVNs. Make an airstrike on the whole area."

Sanders removed a couple of packs of cigarettes from his pack, stuffing them into his pocket, and then looked hard at the young lieutenant.

"No. If they wanted to kill us, they would've hit us by now. Stay here. Remember, twenty-four hours, then leave. Understand?"

Reluctantly, McWaters nodded.

"How do you know he's going to let you go?"

"I don't." Sanders looked around for a minute and then walked out across the clearing as the sun burst once more from behind the clouds.

As Sanders walked into the shadows beneath the trees he saw, as he had already guessed, perhaps a dozen VC laying behind trees and bushes. There may have been still more scattered around. He saw that many of them were teenagers, and one or two looked no more than twelve. Several carried long tubes of cotton filled with rice, what the VC called "elephant's intestines," slung crossways over the shoulder. Two of the black uniformed VC came forward, one gesturing the others to fall back. This man was evidently an officer and carried an automatic pistol of a type Sanders had never seen before. The officer produced a black cloth and tied it tightly around Sanders's eyes. He felt hands holding his arms, guiding him. He was pushed forward and he felt his hand placed on the shoulder of a man in front.

They walked for what seemed several hours. But more than once Sanders felt he was deliberately being led in a circle. He sensed it was night, the air was chill. Once they stopped for several minutes with no one moving, listening perhaps for the sound of pursuit or aircraft.

Most of the time, the ground beneath Sanders's feet seemed hard-packed like a trail, but they suddenly swung off over some rough ground. The Vietnamese came to a halt. The blindfold was untied. Sanders stood blinking and for a moment he thought they were simply in the middle of the forest, and then a lantern threw a patch of light and he saw the outline of shelters and lean-tos under the trees and the dark shapes of men moving around. There was no fire and no sign of cooking.

Someone motioned him toward a thatch-roofed shelter. He had to stoop to get into it. A man was sitting inside, the bottom half of him lit by an oil lantern, the outline of his head and shoulders in shadow. Sanders squatted down.

"Hello, Jai."

"Lewis. Long time, no see. How the hell are you?" The same voice, the same careful diction. For a moment Sanders thought that only he had aged, had changed through the years.

"Can't complain, Jai. How's yourself?"

"Doing great, Lewis."

"Still at the same job, I see."

"I can say the same."

Sanders reached into his pocket and tossed the packs of cigarettes across.

"Lewis, you do not forget a friend."

"Maybe that's why I'm here, Jai, because I don't forget a friend. I hear you've been doing a job on some of our people."

A match flared, and for an instant he saw half of Lazar's face, a smiling handsome man, and he felt a chill, he supposed it was fear, as if he had seen the face of someone he thought was dead—or a harbinger of death.

A chuckle floated out of the darkness. The cigarette tip glowed, and for a moment, the gleam of an eye.

"I knew they were going to send someone, Lewis. And it did not surprise me when I found out it was you."

"Well, our security's pretty lousy, you know. But we just truck along, doing what we can."

"You people are going to have to do better than that, Lewis."

"Yeah, well, we're learning all the time."

A dark shape loomed in the shelter entrance and a black-pajamaed Vietnamese came in and squatted next to Lazar, staring at the American. The light caught a long, worried-looking face and plastic-rimmed eyeglasses. He muttered something to Lazar. The Eurasian answered curtly. They seemed to argue for a moment and then the other man shrugged and left. Lazar sighed. "That was Duan, the commander of this—ah, unit. The military mind, Lewis, sometimes it never learns."

"I came in alone, Jai, my men are back where you picked me up."

A hand waved acknowledgment in the light of the lantern.

"Good idea to meet me in a temporary camp like this. Keeps me away from the real base, right? That must be quite a complex you've got out there, Jai. It's not far from here I take it?"

"Ah, Lewis, I remember you were very good at this sort of thing. We did well together in the war, yes? Do you remember that convoy we ambushed near Bac Ninh? An entire company. That was a great day."

An image of choking smoke and the air rippling with the intense heat from burning trucks. A man on fire, screaming as he runs into the jungle, and Sanders bathed in sweat as he fired and fired.

"Why are you doing it, Jai?"

A glow of the cigarette. A sound, what was it? Tiredness. An exhalation of breath. The guard, just outside the door, did he move, motion to someone? When did they plan to kill him?

"Lewis, I am surprised at you. You always knew I was a patriotic Vietnamese. This is my nation. The colonial war did not end in nineteen-fifty-four. We are going to win this one, Lewis. Do you think we can just sit and watch that—that murderer Diem and his crazy family rule half our country?" Lazar was speaking carefully, his melodious voice hardly a whisper. "The election was stopped. The Geneva Accords said there should have been a vote to unite the country."

"A vote? There was a vote in the South. How much voting have you had in the North?"

"Ho would have won the election, Lewis. Diem knew that."

"I wouldn't know."

"And what are you here for, Lewis?"

"Helping out. Helping to give the people here in the South a chance to decide their own fate."

Lazar seemed to relax, and Sanders could detect a smile in the dim light.

"You Americans. You profess not to know anything about politics but you are the most political people in the world." Lazar stubbed out the cigarette. "Anyway, what are you Americans going to do with my country? Now that you are here helping us."

"I think, Jai, that for starters we're not going to make it easy for Uncle Ho."

They sat silently for a moment, both letting the silence become strained.

"Must I kill you, Lewis?" The voice finally floated out of the darkness. And then Lazar answered his own question, his voice now tired and resigned as if some sort of debate had been going on for a long time. "I think if I do not, you will kill me."

And Sanders knew that he was hearing his death sentence.

"Jai," he said slowly, "stop the killing, these assassinations of Americans. It's terrorism, Jai, not war. It can only be counterproductive to your cause. The United States is a giant that doesn't like to be stung. If you go on with this, we're going to react and many Vietnamese are bound to get hurt."

"Is that what you came here for? To tell me to stop these—legitimate attacks on our country's invaders?"

"I thought perhaps, for old times' sake, I could impress upon you that it can only end in disaster. Give you an out."

"An out. An out," Lazar exploded with rage. In the dim light Sanders could see his chest heaving. "You come into my country. You tell me how I am supposed to fight for our freedom from a tyrant and an imperialist colonizer, and you offer me an out."

The guard outside the door stirred nervously. Sanders heard faint footfalls as some VC approached. There was a mutter of voices. Sanders knew his life was hanging by the merest thread.

Lazar, calmer now, lit another cigarette. "Perhaps there is something you can do for me." The hand holding the cigarette rested in the pool of light.

Sanders waited, his heart pounding. A faint hope of reprieve.

"Take a message from us to your Ambassador Vossenack. Tell him that the Central Committee of the National Liberation Front is willing to negotiate with the Diem regime." The fingers on the hand spread wide. "To achieve a peaceful settlement to this . . . state of insurgency. Providing . . . providing the Diem government acknowledges the NLF as a legitimate expression of the Vietnamese people and with the precondition that we—and the Buddhists—are included in a coalition government until formal, internationally supervised elections have taken place."

Sanders snorted. "That's cold potatoes, Jai. It's nothing new. What authority do you have to offer this plan, anyway?"

"This comes from the top. From the Regional Committee and Hanoi."

"Why me? Hanoi can get this sort of thing passed on through any neutral embassy in the world. The Swiss would be glad to do it."

"Let us say this is another avenue. A more direct route than others we can use or have used in the past. What could be closer to our goal than the office of the American ambassador in Saigon? But there is more." Cigarette smoke swirled slowly in the light of the lantern, almost obscuring even the shadowy image beyond the light. "This proposal will also be presented to the Saigon government by the Self-Determination Movement. We expect a dozen or more major intellectual voices in Saigon—artists, academics, lawyers—to petition for direct negotiation with the NLF on this proposal and an immediate return to the Geneva Accords. These individuals will campaign both in Saigon and in the provincial capitals, and we expect the petition will receive international publicity. To show our good faith we are informing your government of this development in advance so that it will have time to formulate a response. Time is of the essence to both our sides."

Sanders shrugged. "Vossenack will clear this with Washington before he says a word to the South Vietnamese government."

"Of course. The Americans are the key to any peace in Vietnam. It is obviously in their interest, too."

"Okay. I'll pass it on. But I think you have an exaggerated sense of how much influence the United States has with the government of South Vietnam."

"Thank you, Lewis. I appreciate this personally. Now I will not have to use some poor captured American military adviser. But it is late." The hand turned so that Lazar could read a large stainless-steel watch. "You probably wish to get back to your comrades. I will have some of my men escort you."

"Jai," Sanders leaned forward, his voice dropping, "you might consider . . . if things got—rough for you, of course . . . coming over to us. You'd receive a very . . . favorable reception, and you'd have our protection."

Beyond the light, the shadowy image seemed to ponder this for a moment, not saying anything.

Sanders stirred, trying to rise to his feet. He stumbled for a moment, throwing out his hand to steady himself. His hand came down on the lantern, tilting it suddenly so that it shone upward into Lazar's face. He looked the same as Sanders remembered. A little older, perhaps, but the same Jai. The Eurasian smiled.

"The legs getting old, Lewis?"

They walked outside. Sanders could see the dark shapes of sentries. Somewhere there was a cackle of laughter and some coughing. Lazar called softly in Vietnamese, and three men appeared, the outline of their floppy hats and slung rifles black against the sky. Lazar gave them an order, and they prepared to leave.

"Good-bye, my friend. It was good to see you again." Lazar held out his hand. "We fought a good war together."

"Take care, Jai. Don't let them leave you holding the bag."

"Holding the bag. I remember you used to say that in the war. I had forgotten. But, as you also often said, it is my ballgame."

Sanders grinned as he was blindfolded again. "I had a lot of great sayings, didn't I?"

They led him back over the same country to where

McWaters, Chu, and Le were still waiting. And as he walked along the trail, still expecting a bullet in the back at any moment, he knew that the options were over. Perhaps, in a way, he was a fool to have imagined that there could have been any option but one. From now on—the realization still struck him with a cold finality—there were no more choices. Lazar was not going to stop the killings. Perhaps he could not stop even if he wanted to. Now it was certain. One of them would die. And it was not going to be Lewis J. Sanders.

"You're a fool to let him go," said the battalion commander. "He intends to kill you. And why did you inform him about the petition? My understanding was that it should not be discussed at present. Not all the arrangements have been made. As for the proposal itself, you do not have the authority to deal with the Americans—besides the fact that Diem will not consider it and the Americans will not believe it. It's a useless gesture."

The battalion commander was a survivor. He had been fighting since he was ten years old, making booby traps by sticking bamboo spikes through pieces of rubber tire.

"Yes, comrade commander, the proposal is absurd. But I had to make it appear I had some reason to let Sanders go. Why? Because if we kill him now the Americans will only send someone else. Now I know who my enemy is. I can eliminate him when the time comes. Right now, I need time. Besides," he added, "it is part of our strategy: *Danh va dam, dam va danh* [fighting and talking, talking and fighting]." To the Vietcong, peace discussions were an integral part of warfare, with ultimate victory always the goal.

"Well, commissar," the battalion commander shrugged in resignation, "I hope the comrade general agrees with you."

"Duan, you worry too much."

The temporary shelters had been torn down, and the VC were forming up for the march back to the main base. An officer moved along the ranks, patting men on the shoulder. Commands were called and scouts trotted out into the darkness.

"Comrade commissar," said the battalion commander, "I have seen the fate of many men who did not worry enough." His face was caught for an instant in the light from a candle. He was a particularly doleful-looking man, gaunt and haggard, with his cheekbones protruding from his face. Like a man who had just come through a hard winter, thought Lazar, and he suppressed a smile—Lewis used to say that.

"We won't have trouble with Sanders, Duan, never fear." Lazar took a drag on his American cigarette. Some things were regrettable, of course, but the discipline of the revolution was unrelenting. Why then did he have the gnawing coldness inside him? Because there was no turning back? He stared off into the blackness, wondering at the inexplicable sadness of it all.

10

"Of course," said Ambassador Vossenack, "Lazar now realizes that Sanders is the one he has to worry about. It might be opportune for us to make sure he continues to believe that."

"I agree," said Schack. The CIA's Saigon Station Chief was a balding, dark-haired man, overweight, wearing a rumpled wash-and-wear suit. His eyes, imbedded in deep black circles, looked sadly out of a sallow, mottled complexion. "It's better that he keeps his mind on Sanders, while our other asset maintains contact."

"How is the good colonel?"

"Keeps angling for more money."

"Don't they all?"

The three men laughed. They were in the Station Chief's office. A spacious room, it was actually part of a suite, much bigger than would be expected for someone with the rather innocuous embassy title of "agricultural counselor." Surprisingly, however, it was quite bare. It was hard to tell, in fact, if the office was being used. No framed pictures. No memorabilia. Not even a nameplate on the door. The standard issue State Department desk had only a telephone, an embassy directory, and squarely centered, a desk pad. One or two books, English-Vietnamese dictionaries, were in a bookcase against the wall. The room had a musty smell.

"In the meantime, General Bachelor, I believe this is too good an opportunity to let pass."

The third man, General Bachelor, head of MACV, was

a complete contrast to the CIA Station Chief. Tall, with a distinguished air helped by his silvery sideburns and trim moustache, the general had a vibrant healthy look as if he had just finished a long vacation at a health resort. Bachelor nodded. "I'll get hold of the III Corps area commander, General Vien. An ARVN ranger battalion should do it. We'll sanitize the whole area."

"Where is Sanders now?" said the CIA man.

"Back at his Chinese hotel, believe it or not. Mc-Waters at least has more sense. He's at BOQ."

The CIA man shook his head. "Sorry to hear that Sanders has gone native on us. I'd better let Hoyt and Schofield know."

"Well, the Agency can't say I didn't warn it," said Vossenack. He glanced around satisfactorily.

"Lazar gave no indication of what he was planning?"

"Not according to Sanders."

"You've seen him since he's got back then?"

"Oh, yes. Strolled into my office still in his combat fatigues, smelling of the jungle. Didn't even bother to bathe and change first. I mean, he came right in through the front lobby of the embassy. It really bothered my secretary." The ambassador's jaw tightened. He could still see Sanders arrogantly lounging in one of the Queen Anne guest chairs, his filthy clothes ruining the upholstery. And then there was the condition that Margaret came back in after her trip to Ben Thong. What is going on with everybody here?

"Well, we may have to pull him out," said the CIA man. "We'll see how this mission goes."

"Those ARVN ranger boys are good. We've trained them well," said the general. His white teeth flashed as he smiled, looking off into the distance as if he could see the beauty of the coming action.

"What about this proposal from the VC?"

"Well, I'll pass it on, of course, but it's absurd. We've

already gone over the same ground. But the petition is something new, and we'll have to come up with a response to it. I have the political section working on it now."

"About the other thing," said the CIA man. "I think we can count on Minh, Ba, and possibly Dang."

"It has to look like a Vietnamese show," said Vossenack. He shifted uncomfortably, the subject distasteful. "You know the feeling in Washington right now. We must have deniability."

"We won't be directly involved." The Station Chief wiped his face with an oversize handkerchief. The air conditioning was not working right, and it was hot in the room. "What a climate. I wish my successor luck with the air conditioning." He was taking an early retirement, the result of an ulcer and a nagging wife who wanted to stay in Atlanta.

"But still no real decision."

"Kennedy's people are split. So is the NSC. Talk, talk, talk." The plump CIA man flapped his handkerchief in an effort to dry it. "You know the argument, 'If not the man we've got now, who?'"

"Speaking of—"

"No harm. That's been established. It looks like exile."

"I'm sorry in a way," said the ambassador. "Margaret was so much looking forward to the dedication."

All day the American helicopters, ostensibly part of the South Vietnamese National Army but still painted with the lightning flash insignia of the U.S. Twenty-fifth Infantry Division, had been shuttling between Tan Son Nhut Airport and the jungle about thirty miles north of Saigon, bringing in the Vietnamese rangers. The rangers, bright red scarves, tiger heads painted on their helmets, dashed quickly into the trees as the choppers landed, anxiously urged on by their American advisers—a captain and three sergeants.

By midmorning they had penetrated five miles into the jungle, trying to find Vietcong, who seemed to have vanished. An occasional shot sent everyone ducking for cover, but it always turned out to be a nervous ARVN. Constantly on the move, urging a company commander to make his men move faster or snapping at the heels of a platoon more lackadaisical than the others, the American advisers looked at each other disgustedly. This looked like another operation that was going nowhere.

Sanders had laughed when he had been told by a spit-and-polish major from MACV that he had been ordered to accompany the mission to the spot where he had been contacted by the Vietcong. "They're not there, Major. They're not going to be so stupid as to wait around for us to find them."

"A mission has been set up, and Ambassador Vossenack specifically requested that you accompany the assault. We can clear it with Washington, but we didn't think it was necessary to do that." The major was unsure exactly how to treat this strange-looking civilian.

Irritably, Sanders had briefed American and Vietnamese officers on his meeting with Lazar. The officers had listened eagerly to what he had to say, noted the location he pointed out on the map, and then promptly forgot about him as they worked together on the logistics of transporting a Vietnamese ranger battalion into the field.

Sanders and his team had gone in with the second wave. The LZ came up fast, and they scrambled out of the CH-21 helicopter and walked through the swirling dust past running groups of ARVNs, with Sanders ignoring the shouted commands and the exasperated looks of the American advisers. Before they had taken off from the airport an American soldier had run up with helmets and bullet-proof vests for them. Sanders wasn't wearing either.

Five hours later, there was no sign of the VC, but two rangers had accidentally shot themselves and had been air evacuated and three had been killed by a mine booby trap.

It had gone off with a tremendous explosion about two hundred yards ahead of Sanders and his men. When they inspected the area—a gaping hole in the ground still smoking, three Vietnamese being carried away in shelter halves, and a foot still incongruously in a boot at the lip of the hole—they found it had been made from an American 105 mm howitzer shell set to blow up with the pressure of a foot. Nearby, they found another one rigged with a tripwire, but the fuze was a dud.

The mines slowed the rangers down, the spirit gone out of them. Much of the battalion became scattered through the jungle as groups of men wandered off or hunkered down apathetically. Small knots of ARVN officers gathered then broke apart as the Americans ran up, only to reform again.

Sanders and his group sat together, eating quietly as all around them rangers chattered excitedly. The American captain came up to Sanders wearily.

"Well, we found some old bunkers and lean-tos, but they look as though they've been abandoned for years. You're sure of the area?"

"This is it. They set up a base right around here at the end of World War Two. I'm pretty sure this is where they brought me."

The captain, a wiry man with the lean look of a warrior, watched the slow-moving rangers with exasperation.

"Well, it's going to look good on my report to MACV, but there's not much in the way of real stuff. Look at 'em. And these are some of the best they've got. I should have picked the navy. Would you believe I'm from Annapolis, Maryland." He shook his head tiredly and then strode off, yelling at a Vietnamese officer wearing dark glasses.

McWaters glanced at Chu, but the Vietnamese was staring ahead blankly. "How long do you think we'll be out here?" he asked Sanders. He was wearing a bulletproof vest and helmet and carrying a carbine.

"Oh, we'll fart around here until tomorrow morning and then they'll send the choppers out for us," Sanders replied.

Officers shouted commands, the rangers around them stood up and began to get their equipment together.

"Here we go again. I should've told them I met Lazar in the bar of the Continental Hotel."

There was a sudden crackle of gunfire in the distance. Orders were shouted excitedly. Soldiers cautiously moved off through the trees. Ahead, there was the explosion of mortars and the rip of machine-gun fire. As suddenly as it had started, the firing stopped. Six minutes later, Sanders and his men were looking down at the bodies of two black-clad VC. Three rangers had been wounded and were being bandaged nearby.

"Scouts probably. Left behind to see what we did," said Sanders.

McWaters was struck by how young they were. Oddly, he suddenly thought of what they would be doing if they were Americans. Watching "Rawhide" on television. Washing the family car.

"Look at this." Sanders picked up one of the VC's weapons, an American .30-caliber M-1 carbine. "It's a handmade copy. See the machine marks."

"How about this one," exclaimed McWaters.

The other VC had been carrying an old bolt-action rifle. It had Russian markings. They examined the weapons with awe.

The American adviser tipped his helmet back. "That's probably all we're going to see of them this trip."

"There's always a next time, Captain," said Sanders. He turned the carbine over in his hands, thinking of the ingenuity and the dedication. A circle of ARVNs stared at him as if he had some Western magic that explained it all. He looked around at the jungle. Incredible, he thought, and for the first time the magnitude of the struggle with the Vietcong dawned on him. It shook him to realize that somewhere out there, a man was probably planning his death.

11

THE VIETNAMESE SECURITY chief was worried. Refugees had been drifting into the village, all young men, a few here, one or two there. But who were they? Where were they from? Their stories seemed suspiciously alike. "I am from the village of Tan Thong Hoi. It was destroyed by soldiers." "I am from the village of Phu An. Soldiers came one day and burned it." Unusual. Very unusual. "What happened to your parents, the old people in your village?" The story was the same from all of them. "They died."

The security chief rubbed his face anxiously. Like most of those in the self-defense forces, the *Dan Ve*, he was a Catholic, a refugee from the north. If he reported his suspicions to the government, his life and those of his family would be in immediate danger. The Vietcong would kill them. Stake his head on a pole to warn others. They did just this to the security chief of a village not eight kilometers away. If he did not report it and the government found out the hamlet was sheltering Vietcong, it would be treason. The best that would happen to him would be years in one of Diem's jails, with a high likelihood he would never come out alive. He thought about his wife and his three young children. What would happen to them? What would happen to all of them when the Americans left, as he was sure they would one day? Who would protect them from the Communists? What could the government do to protect the hamlet?

He idly thumbed through the latest directive from the

government in Saigon. The village's taxes were being raised to pay for new construction. He sighed, dropped the pamphlet on his desk, and walked out on the porch of his small thatched house and searched the sky. The monsoon was breaking. A passing storm had left some ragged clouds being slowly scattered by the wind. Beyond the village, the setting sun had tinged the sodden fields a dark red. His smallest child, a girl, was playing in the dirt nearby, humming to herself. He could hear the voices of other children chanting their lessons in the school.

The security chief walked through the village. The original bamboo enclosure had been replaced by heavy poles and interlaced barbed wire, seven strands high. Outside the fence was a wide drainage ditch. A channel had been dug to it from the river so that the ditch was almost filled with water, partially surrounding the hamlet like a moat. Some men were setting up rows of sharpened bamboo stakes, pushing them into the mud at the bottom of the ditch so that they jutted up out of the water. It was a crude but effective defense.

The security chief watched them work. What did he have to protect the hamlet? Fifteen old men and ten boys with worn-out French rifles and an old MAT-49 machine pistol left over from the 1940s. The security chief listened to the voices of the schoolchildren. Perhaps it would be better if he said nothing—for now, of course.

Margaret Vossenack was bored. The talk around the table was stilted, awkward, inhibited by the presence of the two Vietnamese generals and their blank-faced wives, who understood little English. Bud Bailey (why must Robert keep inviting that man?), a boisterous, overweight engineer directing marketing operations for Allied-White, the big American company doing much of the construction at Bien Hoa air base outside of the city, was telling a long story about his football-playing days at Purdue. The story seemed to go on interminably and finally wound up with a description of a drunken brawl in the locker room at the end of a game. The Americans around the table tried to look interested and laughed politely. The Vietnamese stared vacantly at Bailey.

She glanced almost desperately down the table at Robert, who presided at the other end. Between them sat the Vietnamese, Bailey, one of the embassy interpreters, the CIA Station Chief (she never could remember his name) and General Bachelor from MACV.

She tried to guide the conversation to the subject of a Vietnamese cultural mission that was being organized to tour the United States—General Dang's wife was one of the sponsors—but Bailey began to talk to General Bachelor and Robert about progress at the air base, and the Vietnamese women's slow and halting English made Margaret eventually give up.

How tiring it all was really, the same people, the same conversations. Perhaps she and Robert should have had more children. Margaret sipped her drink and wondered if her sister, living in a wealthy suburb of New York, found life more stimulating. The centerpiece of the table was a large bouquet of bright blue flowers. As she looked at them over the rim of her glass, Margaret Vossenack was surprised to find herself thinking of that strange Major Sanders.

Sanders lay on the bed in his small hotel room. It was bare except for the bed, a bedside table, and a chest of drawers. Saigon hotels were gradually replacing their ceiling fans with air conditioners, and the hum of the machine was not quite loud enough to drown out either the noise of the traffic from the street or the sounds of lovemaking in the next room. It was late evening but the traffic still showed no signs of slowing. Sanders picked up a pack of cigarettes from the bedside table and lit one. He had been at a conference on base security at MACV all day, and he was tired, but sleep came slowly. More and more he was finding that he only slept for an hour or so at a stretch before waking with a numb arm or an aching pain in his chest. The pain in his chest was especially bothering him. Now it was a constant dull ache.

The sounds in the next room were reaching a crescendo. Despite Madame Nhu's edict against prostitution, a number of whores in the neighborhood found the hotel's facilities convenient. Sanders lay on the thin mattress, one arm behind his head, trying to blot out the groans of a false orgasm.

His thoughts wandered to his ex-wife. Elizabeth DeCourt was a delicate-looking woman, the daughter of a shipping executive, and an art major at Bryn Mawr with an unexpected talent in mathematics. When he came home from the war, they had moved to Denver, where he could find work as a geologist. She had hated it. She had filled their home with paintings of elderly women and spent hours solving involved cryptograms. Geology did not interest her at all.

He remembered the terrible scene when he told her that he was going back into the army. It was 1950. The United States was sending troops to Korea. "You're not even in the reserves," she sobbed. He tried to explain to her that he had been asked to return to active duty. An evasive telephone call from a Colonel Somebody hinting at his experience in "special operations. Al Schofield mentioned you as a possibility." He had never heard of Al Schofield. Tears running down her face, his wife had slumped in a chair and then seemed to withdraw into herself. When he kissed her good-bye she barely responded. As he walked out the door she said quietly, "Be careful, Lew." When he looked back at her she was gazing listlessly out of the window. It was not until he was in Korea that he received her letter telling him she was pregnant. At first he had been in a rage. He would not have gone back into the army. And then he realized that she knew him better than he would admit to himself. It would not have made any difference. But how could he have explained to her that he hated working for a big oil corporation, that he was only alive when he was leading men in a war—the only time he was testing himself to the utmost. But perhaps his wife had guessed that, and he felt ashamed that she seemed to know him so well. And the knowledge that he had abandoned her stayed with him through the years, so that he would suddenly remember it, and the feeling would plunge him into a lonely depression. And with each year that passed the bitterness seemed to corrode his spirit further.

She had come to see him at Letterman. The day they had given him the Silver Star, the general making a joke as he pinned the medal, along with the Purple Heart, on his bandaged chest, and everyone standing around his bed awkwardly. The general made a few hearty comments and then left quickly, trailed by his aides and the hospital administrators. Lewis had tried to smile at his wife, but she just looked down at him sadly as he grimaced in pain. The baby cried on and on, struggling against her arms. Liz looked with horror around the ward at the heavily bandaged men, the debris of some terrible carnage. Everywhere there were muttered groans. In the next bed, a man with a bandaged face suddenly cried out. A foghorn on San Francisco Bay moaned in the distance like an anguished beast. Finally, she had just shaken her head in bewilderment and fled.

More sounds of sexual combat came through the thin wall. Tonight some customer had a doubleheader. Sanders stubbed out the cigarette and closed his eyes, hoping sleep would stop his thoughts.

Margaret Vossenack beamed at the twenty-eight schoolchildren, all scrubbed faces and white clothes.

"Good morning," she said brightly.

The new schoolteacher repeated her words in Vietnamese, and the children responded. She had been introduced to the new schoolteacher that morning by the mayor, with the smiling nurse translating. A thin, intense man, dressed in the inevitable white shirt and black pants and carrying a briefcase, he had been sent out to teach at Ben Thong by the authorities in Saigon. Margaret had found him to be cold and stiff, which she had at first put down to his fear over the new position and the interest in the hamlet by the wife of the American ambassador.

"Mr. Phong is university graduate and speak some English," said the mayor. He looked uncomfortable for a moment, keeping his gaze away from the schoolteacher. "He has been given second chance by the government."

"Second chance? I don't understand," said Margaret.

"Mr. Phong, unfortunately, was active in subversive terrorist organization that try to destroy government," said the mayor, and the nurse, for the first time, did not smile, "and had to . . . er, be reeducated into democratic way. As a condition of release he must serve government—" he said something hurriedly to the schoolteacher, who answered with a monosyllable, "for ten year," the nurse finished the translation.

While the mayor was talking, Phong had stood stiffly, expressionless, still clutching the briefcase.

"Well, I'm sure he will do very well in Ben Thong," said Margaret uncertainly.

The Vietnamese walked stiffly beside her as they walked to the classroom, and Margaret was conscious of an intense hostility.

"Class, this morning I would like to tell you something

about the government of your country," began Margaret, "and why it's so important for you to appreciate what your great President Diem has done for the Republic of Vietnam. As you know, I am the wife of the American ambassador." She paused for a moment, waiting for Phong to translate, but he stared back at her. Thinking that he was waiting to translate more of what she said, she decided to continue. "The United States feels that—"

Phong suddenly interrupted, speaking in English. "Does not the United States believe in self-determination, Mrs. Vossenack?"

Margaret was stunned for a moment, as much by the discovery that the schoolteacher's English was very good as by the question.

"Well, yes, of course. The United States has always believed in the self-determination of every country."

"Including self-determination for Vietnam?"

"Yes." She was becoming vaguely annoyed. The children stared at the two adults at the front of classroom, sitting in absolute silence. "As I was saying—"

He interrupted her rudely again. "Why doesn't the United States allow self-determination for Vietnam?"

"We have—we do." She was flustered, not knowing where the conversation was leading. "Really, Phong, this is not the time—"

"Why should not this be discussed in a classroom? Is not the classroom the foundation of democracy?"

"Yes, I suppose so, but—"

"The United States stopped free elections throughout Vietnam that were to have taken place according to the Geneva Accords." Phong was quivering with suppressed rage, staring at the American woman, his face beaded with sweat. Incongruously, he still gripped the briefcase as if he were waiting for a bus that might pass through the classroom. "What right has the United States and the false Diem regime to do this? Why does the great nation of the United States of America support the dictatorship of the Diem family? My country has been fighting for freedom for a thousand years. Why does the United States proclaim its support of self-determination to the world, and then deny Vietnam its freedom by supporting the colonial ambitions of France?" Phong was almost shouting now. Veins stood out on his neck, his face flushed red.

Margaret wilted under the barrage of questions. She stared back at the grave eyes of the children, her mind in a turmoil, feeling waves of embarrassment and helplessness.

"American imperialists have replaced the French in enslaving the southern part of our country through a disguised colonial regime," the schoolteacher's voice shouted on. His voice was mechanical, reciting as if by rote. "They and their stooge, the Diem administration, have been responsible for the exploitation of our compatriots—"

"Phong," said Margaret, weakly, "this is rude and inappropriate—" She turned and stumbled from the room, the voice of the schoolteacher still chanting, his eyes wide and a look of triumph on his twisted face, "They maneuver to permanently divide our country and to turn its southern part into a military base in preparation for war in Southeast Asia—"

Margaret found herself outside the schoolroom, gasping for breath, almost vomiting from the burning shame and embarrassment. She stood for a moment, looking ahead blindly in the hot, humid air. Two villagers walked past, staring curiously at her, and she tried to pull herself together. She supposed Phong was a Communist and should be turned in, but that would mean more imprisonment for him, possibly torture and death—she was under no illusion about the treatment of prisoners by the

Diem government. She stood wondering if she could live with that.

"Softie," she growled at herself. She began to walk toward the mayor's office and then stopped. Perhaps she could reason with Phong, work with him to show that Americans were not the aggressors he believed them to be. Wasn't that better than putting people in jail—or worse? She suddenly thought of Sanders and his nearby camp. Her steps took her toward the path leading to the river. Perhaps she would discuss it with the major. She wiped her forehead with her handkerchief, wondered how she looked. She had left her purse in the car. Oh, well.

"Hello," Margaret called almost timidly as she approached the sandbagged bunker. At first the place looked abandoned. Then a voice answered hello. On the other side of the low fortification, sitting with his back to a log, was Lieutenant McWaters. Bare to the waist, he had a writing pad on his knee and was looking at her with a startled expression.

"Oh, Lieutenant McWaters. I thought I recognized you when I was here before. I'm Margaret Vossenack. You may remember, we met at an embassy reception some weeks ago."

"Yes, ma'am," said the lieutenant. He stood up clumsily, and she wondered why he looked strangely toward the bunker.

"I was looking for Major Sanders," Margaret smiled. "Is he here?"

"No, ma'am. The—er, major is in the city. We expect him out tomorrow."

"Well, perhaps you'll tell him I just dropped by to say hello. I was in the village—" Margaret suddenly stopped. From the bunker came the sound of a girl's laugh. And then some unmistakable sounds that one did not normally hear in a bunker, even one in the paddy fields of

Vietnam. Then another giggle. Margaret froze. She walked swiftly over to the low doorway and then backed away, red with embarrassment. The glimpse of bare thighs and breasts was sufficient.

"I see I'm intruding," she said stiffly. McWaters, abashed, was looking down on the ground. She turned to go when a thought struck her. "Who are they, Mr. McWaters?"

"Oh, that's just Chu and Le, Mrs. Vossenack."

"No, I mean the women."

McWaters seemed to find it difficult to swallow. Whatever he had been writing was now crumpled into a ball.

"Did they come from the hamlet?" Her tone was icy.

"I think—er, well I think so." McWaters looked miserable.

Margaret went red with anger. "I won't have you corrupting the people in this village, Lieutenant. This is an outrage. Where is Major Sanders now? I demand that you tell me or I'll go directly to the ambassador."

McWaters seemed to struggle with the question and finally said, "He's at a hotel called the Great Asia—it's Chinese—just off Lam Son Square, Mrs. Vossenack. That's all I know."

Margaret stormed back to her waiting limousine, leaving the village officials looking bewildered and the MPs shrugging. Near the embassy she dismissed the large automobile and took a pedicab. She felt hurt and angry, but it was the first time she had been out alone on the streets of Saigon, and for a moment she stopped feeling angry and just enjoyed the extraordinary sights of a large city in Southeast Asia. She looked around with delight at the tremendous flow of people, the constant uproar and noise. White uniformed police directed traffic, somehow seeing order in the chaos. Old women gaped at her, their mouths like slashed red wounds from the juice of betel nuts. Street stalls sold everything imaginable—she glimpsed neat stacks of canned V-8 Juice and Polaroid cameras alongside hair spray and platform shoes. Farmers in from the countryside jogged past carrying huge wicker baskets full of vegetables, balancing one at each end of long bamboo poles. Margaret smiled at the exaggerated gait of pregnant Vietnamese women, stomachs extended, their arms hanging loosely behind them.

The pedicab driver seemed to find his way without hesitation and grinned lasciviously at her as he stopped outside a small three-story hotel above a bar, with flapping banners hung from its balconies advertising hair cream and cigarettes. Inside the dim foyer, a skinny Chinese popped up from behind the desk.

"I would like the room number of one of your guests. A Major Sanders," said Margaret, feeling a little ridiculous.

The Chinese laughed delightedly.

"Oh, yes. Oh, yes. Give numba'. Give numba'." He stood back and looked at the slots behind the desk grandly. He only had nine of them.

"Ah, yes." From the vast number of guests in the establishment, he was finally able to pin down Sanders's room number.

"Numba'," the Chinese seemed to do some calculating in his head, "eight." He beamed. He leaned over the counter and watched her walk up the stairs, grinning with delight. Margaret was beginning to have second thoughts. Sanders's room was on the top floor of the hotel. The dim hallway had windows open at both ends and was lit by a single naked bulb. A baby was crying somewhere. She hesitated and then knocked at the door. It opened so quickly that it almost threw her off balance. Sanders stood gazing at her. His shirt was off, and she deliberately avoided looking at the massive chest with its terrible scar. His hair was disheveled and wet as if he had just taken a shower, although it was four in the afternoon.

"Major Sanders, I have just been out at your, er, campsite, and something has come to my attention that I feel should be discussed immediately," she said, trying to keep her tone neutral.

"Come in, Mrs. Vossenack," his voice low and gravelly. He held the door open for her. She walked in carefully almost expecting to see a harem of ravished virgins. Instead she saw a drab, small room with a square of worn carpet and a tiny bathroom. Water was dripping from one of the faucets. She wondered why he chose a hotel like this instead of one of the better places.

"The reason why I came, Mr. Sanders—I mean Major Sanders—" She was conscious of that straight unblinking gaze. He walked over to a shirt draped over the back of a chair and pulled it on.

"The reason I came here is," she began again, "is that you must stop your men *using*—I believe I can define it as that—the village girls. There are many other places in Vietnam where they can do that sort of thing. That village is a model for other hamlets in Vietnam. I cannot allow this sort of—corrupt behavior to go on in association with the name of the United States."

"Did you have a word with the women?"

"Well, no, I left in a, er, hurry."

"Do you think my men forced them to screw?"

An image of grins and white teeth in the darkness.

"I wish you wouldn't use that word, Major Sanders. But, well, no, I suppose they didn't."

"Then what do you want from me?"

"They are your men, Major. You are responsible for their behavior."

Sanders sighed and walked over to a window, his hands in his pockets.

"I see. I'm going to tell Vietnamese, grown men in

their own country, how they're supposed to conduct themselves because Americans just don't like their sexual practices. We don't do things like that, is that it?"

"I—I just can't have this sort of thing going on in the hamlet." Margaret said it with what she hoped was flat finality.

Sanders walked over to a tray on the bedside table.

"Drink, Mrs. Vossenack? I've only got whisky."

She was startled for the moment. "Well, all right, thank you."

He took some ice from a bucket and dropped it into two glasses and splashed in some liquor.

"We'll be leaving in a day or so, Mrs. Vossenack. No need to worry. It was sort of a graduation present."

"It seems . . ."

"Disgustingly immoral," he smiled, holding the glasses.

"It's not that, Major. I'm no prude. You can't be married to an army general without hearing a lot of what goes on in life. It's just that the village—the village is important to me."

He looked down at the drinks, nodding.

"Why did you really come here, Mrs. Vossenack?"

"Why, about your men, of course."

"I thought perhaps you came to see me."

"You presume a lot, Mr. Sanders, I—"

He suddenly put the two glasses back on the tray and kissed her, pulling her into his arms one hand behind her head. For a moment she seemed to hang in his arms loosely as if all her strength had left her. He gently moved her toward the bed.

"No. Stop." She struggled to be free. Suddenly she was afraid of the huge man with the massive arms and shoulders.

For a moment he held on to her, and then reluctantly let her go. "We're both consenting adults, lady, but if you just came here for some slumming, you haven't seen it all yet. The girls rent the next room by the hour. You might want to take some notes."

She pushed a strand of hair back out of her eyes and searched wildly for her purse. It was on the floor. He made no move to pick it up for her. She grabbed it, pulled open the door, and rushed out. As she slammed it behind her it caught her dress, and she had to open the door again to free herself. She ran down the stairs blindly. The Chinese man behind the desk cackled and seemed to find things immensely funny.

"Quickie, quick," he chortled.

"Oh, go and—and stuff your chop suey," she yelled back.

His laughter still ringing in her ears, Margaret found herself on the sidewalk, looking desperately for a pedicab. Her eyes filled with hot tears of embarrassment and guilt. It was only later that she realized she had forgotten all about the schoolteacher, but by then it hardly seemed to matter.

Thunder rumbled across the forest, but the rain did little to drive away the deadening heat. Lazar sat at the table in his bunker, going over the notes he had written. It was all there. He felt a fierce exultation. Times, schedules, number of men, weapons. Information brought in slowly, patiently by spies and informers. It was coming together like a mosaic. The pieces fitting each other, slowly forming a picture that astounded him with its clarity. It would be a supreme act, the only real act a patriot can make for his country. The only way his life would have a purpose—in fact, the culmination, the very apogee of his existence. His name would be in the history books alongside the other great patriots. Medals? They would be meaningless. What class of Military Victory Medal could be awarded for what he was about to do? He laughed, his face glistening in the heat. They would revere him. Schoolchildren would sing his name. No longer the pariah, the man with the tainted past. He would be free.

He got up and paced the room, then walked outside the dugout. Earth and sky seemed joined in the darkness, the wind roaring in the trees. He needed time. The latest message from the general had been evasive, hinting at problems of "coordination" with the Regional Committee. The Committee was displeased with him. That was now obvious. The battalion commander had reported his failure to kill Sanders, a dangerous American spy, as well as giving the American the information about the forthcoming petition drive. There was probably an investigation being conducted, and he would not be told about it until someone came to arrest him. Something must be done to keep their attention away from his mission—some operation to give him time to make his final arrangements, to put the last stone into place. The mission. Only that was important. It had to succeed.

He walked back inside and studied the wall map, searching. He went to the table and flipped through a sheath of papers, noting a recent report. Information obtained from a police colonel in Saigon who had contact with the American CIA. He looked again at the map. Yes, it would work. Lazar smiled and stared at the point on the wrinkled, rain-spotted paper.

"Of course, it's too bad he didn't take care of the bastard when he had the opportunity." The deputy director's gold Rolex watch flashed in a beam of sunlight from the tall windows as he swiveled his leather chair.

"It's unlikely he could do much without actually trying to throttle the man. We didn't ask him to commit suicide."

"Hm?" Hoyt did not seem to hear.

"I think he deserves another chance," said Felix. "At least he got close to him."

"Yes, but Schack says that our major seems to have got a touch of the sun y'know." His British accent was quite good. "Living with the natives and all that. And what's more the ambassador doesn't like it."

Felix shrugged. "Sanders is an independent operative. We knew that when we hired him. As for Vossenack. Well . . ." He left the sentence unfinished.

Hoyt smiled at his wall of photographs. "Another chance," he said slowly. The administration was becoming increasingly concerned about Vietnam. It was front-page news and there was an election on the way. Having the right assets was the key. It was all a question of balancing your assets, keeping things in motion.

"There's no one else, is there?"

"There were originally twelve members of Sanders's OSS team who parachuted into Vietnam. Four were killed in action, one died later of wounds. Of the remaining seven, all have died since the war for one reason or another except Sanders, one man who is a severe alcoholic in a VA hospital and no use to us, and one man we think is in Alaska but we can't find."

"So that leaves us with Sanders." Hoyt lounged back in his chair. He must get one of himself with the attorney general. "Well, Felix, if you want to give him another chance, give him one. He's your responsibility, of course. The ball, as they say, is now firmly in your court. Schack's on his way home. And you, dear fellow, now have the honors." The deputy director glanced at his watch. "Oh, by the way. We must have you and that pretty wife of yours out to the farm one weekend soon."

"We'll look forward to it," said Felix.

12

THE AMERICANS CALLED it Firebase Bravo. To the French and Vietnamese it was A Shau. It was situated on a ridge near the radius of several valleys, a site that gave it command of a wide expanse of territory. An old French fort, not much to see, really, it had a stone and concrete tower about twenty feet high, several thatched-roof bungalows, and log and sandbag emplacements, all surrounded by a double fence of barbed wire. Scrub and bush had been cleared about fifty feet back from the outer fence. From the air, the base looked barren and deserted.

To the American seven-man Special Forces team that "advised" the one hundred Civilian Irregular Defense Group Vietnamese that garrisoned the post, however, the importance of Firebase Bravo rested not so much on its strategic geographic position as on its twenty-four-channel VHF radio setup with its thirty-five-foot mast and the three Signal Corps technicians who operated it. Bravo was an important communications link between the American command in Saigon and Special Forces posts like this one strung along the central highlands up to the DMZ. It also handled embassy radio traffic north to the U.S. consulates in Hue and Danang.

In late October 1963, the Special Forces team at Bravo was temporarily down to five men. Its commander, Lieutenant Ellis Boxhill, twenty-seven years old, a rangy blond man from Abilene, Texas, had just evacuated his intelligence NCO, who had a bad ear infection. Another man was due to return from an emergency leave in Hawaii. All travel in and out of the isolated post was by helicopter. Boxhill, an energetic, competent officer, kept his small team of elite soldiers on its toes, constantly setting up training exercises with the CIDG force. But the Vietnamese seemed to move at their own pace, which one Westerner likened to "oozing oil." Life was tedious at Firebase Bravo. A boredom that inevitably dulled the fine edge of alertness.

For three days the Vietcong battalion, about 250 men, many of them no more than teenage boys, led by commissar Jai Lazar and commander Duan had been maneuvering itself into position for an assault on Firebase Bravo. Stealthily working their way forward at night, the VC had set up two recoilless rifles and several mortars on a low ridge, little more than a hump in the ground, less than one hundred yards from the post. A platoon of sappers was now within seventy feet of the wire. Even the VC marveled that they had not been seen so far.

Lazar scanned the base through his binoculars from the cover of some dense bushes.

"Not much movement. They have some men in the emplacements over on the left. Doesn't seem to be anyone in the gun pits in the front there. I wonder if they have someone at the top of the tower."

"Most of them are inside. We will have to be lucky with our first hits." Duan, laying near him, was sweating, his eyeglasses streaked with dirt.

Lazar glanced at his watch and then looked around at the tense rows of VC, their young faces blank. How many of them will die tonight? He pushed the thought out of his mind. The sun was low on the horizon, casting deep shadows across the nearby valleys. Distant hills trailed white threads of cloud. The men at the recoilless rifles and mortars were waiting expectantly. Forty-five minutes. He nodded at Duan, who began to work his way over to the left. Lazar wiped the sweat from his face with his scarf. This was an important step to his mission. A successful raid at A Shau and the Regional Committee could do little against him. He began to count the minutes.

The first indication that the garrison at Firebase Bravo received of a VC attack was a recoilless rifle round that slammed into the radio hut, destroying the radio and killing an American Signal Corps specialist who had been reading an old copy of *Playboy*. VC sappers ran forward and exploded charges under the wire, cutting a wide hole in the outer ring. Small-arms fire swept the compound. Recoilless rifle shells exploded against the tower. As the CIDG men ran panic-stricken from their huts, mortar shells exploded, chopping them down in bunches.

But the inner ring of wire proved to be a more difficult barrier for the VC sappers. As they ran forward with explosives in long bamboo tubes, a machine gun manned by two Special Forces men began to cut them down. Lieutenant Boxhill, blood running from a cut over his eye, rallied the CIDG. The Vietnamese began to return the fire.

"We need some more men on the right," Boxhill screamed to his operations sergeant. The NCO ran, waving a group of Vietnamese forward. Tracers seemed to sail up eerily into the darkness. The compound was lit by the flashes of exploding shells.

"Let's get some light out there," the lieutenant yelled. Flares began to pop out in the sky, bathing the area with an intense white light, revealing the VC sappers trying desperately to explode a hole through the inner ring of wire. Boxhill, crouching in his sandbagged command emplacement, began to fire steadiy with his AR-15, dropping one black-clad VC after another. Light, short, and easy to maintain, the AR-15 has a cyclic fire rate of seven hundred rounds of 5.56 mm ammunition per minute. The bullet tumbles when it enters a human being, causing devastating wounds.

Mortar fire bracketed the sandbagged bunker, shells from the recoilless rifles exploded against the emplacements. A Special Forces soldier, a useless arm dangling by a thread, reeled through the command post door and then collapsed.

"The radio's out," screamed one of the Signal Corps technicians.

"Watch the wire. Don't let 'em get through the wire." Boxhill fired desperately. More and more CIDG men, many of them pinned down in a drainage ditch, were hit by the intense fire from outside the perimeter.

The operations sergeant raced through a hail of bullets and dived in through the open doorway.

"There must be hundreds of them out there." He was gasping, shaken. "They're going to get through the wire any minute."

Boxhill thought desperately. Then he saw the 105 mm howitzer. It had been airlifted in months ago, and had never been fired at a target. The Special Forces team had generally regarded it as a nuisance because it required constant cleaning. The gun sat in a sandbagged pit, two dead Vietnamese sprawled beside it, about twenty yards from the command bunker. Suddenly, Boxhill called to his operations sergeant.

"Jack, come with me."

They ran into the ammunition storeroom at the back of the bunker. Boxhill searched through the boxes desperately as the operations sergeant watched perplexed.

"What the hell are we looking for?"

"Here it is." Boxhill was pulling out a large ordnance box. "Help me with this." They knocked off the lid. Inside were three howitzer shells. They were a new type that had been delivered to the post just the week before.

"Here, grab one quick."

The two Special Forces men hefted the shells and ran out. Outside, they heard whistles blowing. They were just in time. The enemy sappers had finally succeeded in blowing a hole in the second row of wire. A swarm of black-clad Vietcong ran forward.

Boxhill set the first shell fuze for point-blank range. The howitzer roared. A second later the shell exploded right over the mass of VC. There was a loud buzzing and crackling noise. Packed inside the shell were thousands of flechettes, inch-and-a-half-long metal barbs. The deadly arrows rained down on the packed Vietcong and devastated them. They fell in waves, dozens screaming in agony. Some had their weapons pinned to them by the barbs. The ground was covered with bodies. A few black-clad figures staggered forward only to be cut down by machine gun and rifle fire from the cheering CIDG force. Outside the wire, Lazar stared in stunned disbelief.

"Duan," he screamed, "we've got to try again." The battalion commander, laying on the ground, blood streaking his black uniform, hesitated, staring at the commissar.

"Do it," yelled Lazar.

Another group surged toward the gap in the wire.

"Here they come again. Let's give 'em another one," said Boxhill.

Again, the howitzer shell exploded above the VC, cutting them down like a scythe. Their bodies were stacked around the gap in the wire. A few managed to get into the compound but were almost immediately shot and bayoneted. The survivors reeled back. They had had enough. The battalion had been decimated. Shocked, blundering through thorny bushes, Lazar ran from the terrible carnage. He collided with another man. It was Duan. Glasses broken, blood streaming from his ear, the battalion commander snarled something at him and rushed off. Lazar looked back dazedly at the piles of dead illuminated in the white flares that continued to burst above. He staggered off into the bush, almost in a stupor, the screams of the wounded still vibrating in his head. The raid had failed. He would be held accountable. There was only one place he could go for safety. Now the mission was all he had left.

13

IT WAS AN immense building with a domed metal roof, a circle sliced in half like a jumbo-sized Quonset hut from World War Two. A guard unlocked the door and inside they saw a corridor, glaring white from hanging fluorescent lamps, running down the entire center of the building. The light threw no shadows. Air conditioning seemed to make the building icy cold. The corridor was lined with metal doors, each with a small glass-and-chicken-wire-covered aperture. About halfway down the corridor the guard stopped before a door and unlocked it. A bracket held a small white card with a name scrawled on it.

The cell was tiny, perhaps forty square feet. A bench, no more than a plywood board, was set against one wall. A man was sitting on it. The prisoner was young, barely out of his teens. There was a bandage dressing around his leg that looked as though it needed changing. He was still dressed in torn and dirty black pajamas.

"This is the one," said the MP captain.

"They captured him at Firebase Bravo?"

"Yup. The VC carried off most of their wounded but we have a few. This one wasn't too badly hurt. He may have been faking it. We figured he could tell us something so we didn't turn him over to the ARVNs."

Sanders looked around. The cell was too small to hold all of them.

"Well, we need to borrow him for a while, and we'll have to take him out of here."

The captain shrugged. "Okay with me. He's your responsibility. Just don't let him get away from you."

"We'll use your latrine."

They walked back out into the bright sun and the thundering roar of aircraft rolling along the concrete runways of Bien Hoa air base. A cyclone fence separated the military police compound from the rest of the complex. At that stage of the war, Bien Hoa was nowhere near the huge base it later became, but already it was an important part of the American buildup. They could see the skeletons of buildings pushing up everywhere, and lumbering, camouflage-painted U.S. Air Force transports taking off, spewing black clouds of spent aviation fuel. The smell of kerosene enveloped them as they walked along the gravel path to the one-story latrine building.

With Sanders and McWaters walking ahead, Chu and Le dragged the VC along between them. McWaters glanced back, uneasily.

"Do you think he knows anything about our target?"

"That's what we're going to find out. Firebase Bravo is about three, maybe four, days' march from the area where we had the contact. It's worth a try."

Inside the concrete floored latrine, heavy with the odor of Lysol, urine, and sweating men, Sanders ordered McWaters to stand by the door and keep everyone out.

The husky man turned to the young Vietnamese prisoner and smiled. The prisoner's eyes rolled side to side desperately. He was terrified. A cackle of laughter came from Chu, who had the VC's arms twisted up behind him. Le stood blank faced. For the two Vietnamese this was a routine exercise. McWaters leaned against the wall and stared at the floor. He refused to let himself think about what was coming.

"Ask him how long he's been in the People's Liberation Army."

A sharp question from Chu.

"Three year."

Slowly, almost casually, Sanders asked more questions. The prisoner's rank, his village, his parents' names. The Vietcong hung his head and mumbled his replies.

"Where's his home base?"

Silence. Chu suddenly punched the VC hard in the stomach, screaming the question at him. The prisoner went down on his knees.

"*Troi oi!*" the gasping cry.

Le almost casually slammed him across the face with the back of his hand. Blood trickled down from the VC's nose.

"Ask him again." Sanders looked on impassively. McWaters felt bile rising in his throat. He stared at the grain beneath the white paint on the latrine door. What was it all coming to? Where will we end? He tried to block out the sound of punches hitting a human body. The grunts of the men working over the prisoner.

"Ask him again."

Chu grabbed the VC's hair and jerked back his head. A choking gabble came from the man's throat.

Sanders took a map out of his pocket and unfolded it slowly. He squatted on the floor and laid the map out.

"Show me."

The prisoner stared at the map and Chu growled. He pointed to a spot.

"Okay." Sanders's tone was, quiet, soothing. He smiled at the young VC. The man's shirt had been ripped. One of his eyes was closing.

"Ask him the name of his commissar."

The VC answered promptly, but he stared down at the ground, looking evasive.

Sanders smiled. "The son of a bitch is lyin'. Ask him again."

Chu suddenly swung his leg back, and then his knee came forward thudding into the prisoner's kidneys. The young man screamed and sprawled forward as his captors released him, striking his face on the floor with a sickening thud. The two Vietnamese grabbed his arms and jerked him upright. Le grinned and chopped his hand viciously across the VC's nose. With blood almost covering his face now, the VC made gurgling sounds as it ran into his mouth. McWaters placed both his hands on the wall, sure he was going to be sick. The door shuddered as someone tried to come in.

"What the hell's going on in there?"

"Keep out, goddamn it," yelled the lieutenant. Boots retreated down the hall.

"Ask him again. His commissar?"

Chu began to slap the VC methodically, bouncing the man's head from side to side, all the time screaming the question at him.

The VC gasped something.

"What? I didn't hear him."

Chu stopped the beating. The prisoner choked, groaned something again and spat blood from his mouth. Through swollen lips, he mumbled, "La-zar."

Chu and Le held the man's arms.

"Okay," said Sanders, offhandedly. "That does it. Take him back to the cell."

Legs dragging, the VC was hauled from the latrine, and McWaters heard his bare feet slapping against the concrete as he was half carried down the hall.

"Did you have to do that?"

"Why, Mr. McWaters, you mean they didn't teach an officer and a gentleman like you such nasty things in ROTC at Princeton? Does it offend you? Perhaps you'd rather rush right off back to school and get a fuckin' MBA or something."

"Torture is immoral, illegal, and disgusting. And repugnant to the Armed Forces of the United States." McWaters stared back at Sanders angrily.

"Well hoity fuckin' toity. Killing Americans likewise, preacher. Don't give me any crap like that—peoples' lives are at stake here. When you get back home you can worry about the VC's civil rights. Until then, don't lecture me on bullshit morality in the middle of a war." Sanders glared back at the young naval officer. "Learn, Lieutenant, that when the first man gets killed the rules become hypocrisy. And don't blame Chu, either. One of his brothers was killed in this war, and his father was murdered by the VC for not paying them taxes. As for Le, he'd be shot immediately by the Reds if they could get their hands on him."

McWaters said nothing, still feeling the sour taste in his mouth. Sanders sat on the edge of a wash basin and lit a cigarette. He seemed to calm down.

"There are no rules in this kind of war, Davey. Rules are for West Point graduation dances, and lunches at the officers' club, and briefings for visiting congressmen. There're no rules in this." He glanced at the young officer for a moment almost sympathetically. McWaters suddenly realized that it was the first time Sanders had called him by his given name.

Sanders smiled. "Well, it looks like Lazar has got his ass in a jam. His commie bosses are not going to like this screwup." He folded his arms and thought reflectively. McWaters found himself staring at a pool of blood on the floor, but Sanders seemed to ignore it. The heavyset man stood up. "I think it's time we put some more pressure on old Jai."

The M60 machine gun chattered as the gunner sprayed the area below them, the bullets bending the grass and bamboo like hail.

Small black-clad figures ran for the trees, some pausing to fire back at the helicopters as they descended. Here and there, a body. The long line of Hueys and CH-21s came in like taxis, disgorging ARVNs and then taking off. Tracers arched upward. One of the American helicopters seemed to stagger in the air, taking a hit. It spiraled down and crashed, lying on its side with broken rotor blades like a battered insect. Men fell from its doorways. There were cries for medics. American advisers talked urgently into their radios.

Sanders and McWaters, closely followed by Chu and Le, ran through tall grass behind a knot of Vietnamese soldiers. Bullets snapped above them.

"There!" Sanders pointed. The four men began to fire rapidly, sweeping the treeline. An American adviser led a ragged company of ARVNs across the open ground. They kept firing even as they were swallowed up by the bushes and trees. The noise of machine guns and mortars was incredible. Smoke drifted across the clearing. Behind them, more choppers unloaded troops.

ARVNs ringed the cleared area in front of the bunker as Sanders and his team prepared to rush inside. McWaters pulled a smooth-skinned grenade from his pocket.

"No, if there's someone in there let's try getting him without messing things up too much." Sanders shoved a fresh magazine into his carbine and pulled back the bolt. "Ready?" McWaters nodded. Chu and Le tensed expectantly.

"Go."

They threw themselves inside, crouched, weapons sweeping the area. Then they relaxed.

"Well, take a look around. Check over everything."

"Not a lot of anything," said McWaters. He kicked some cooking pots aside with his foot, then rifled through a neat stack of papers on a shelf. "This stuff'll keep the translators busy." Sanders was staring at an old map pinned to the wall. Le handed him a canvas bag. Inside was some clothing and an automatic pistol.

"A Nambu," Sanders grunted. He laid the items out on the table. An old silver cigarette case. He recognized it as the one Lazar had when they were together in the war. A piece of soap in a plastic container. A steel mirror. Tweezers. Some pamphlets written in Vietnamese, apparently political material. Sanders paused. Interesting. An English-language guidebook of Paris, a 1958 edition and well-thumbed. "What's this?" He unwrapped a small square of silk. Inside was a worn leather wallet. The photo was old and creased, once black and white, now faded to a brownish hue. A water stain covered one corner. There was no inscription.

"I wonder who that could be?" said McWaters, looking over his shoulder. "Looks like a French officer."

Outside the firing was dying away. A few ARVNs looked into the bunker. Officers and NCOs shouted orders. Groups of men ran past.

A sweat-stained American captain came in, grinning.

"Whew, hot in here. Looks like we've hit the jackpot. This is a VC battalion headquarters, maybe even a regiment. There's a heck of a lot of stuff out there. What looks like a barracks. A machine shop. Kitchens. Some kind of hospital. Recoilless rifles, mortars, machine guns, grenades, a big ammunition dump. You name it. There's even a tank—an old Sherman—must have belonged to the French. It doesn't run but they were working on it." He pushed his helmet back, sweat running down his face. "The ARVNs did some interrogating," his eyes skittered away. "Seems they lost a lot of men a short time ago. I bet this is the outfit that attacked Firebase Bravo."

"It is," said Sanders. He still sat on the edge of the table looking down at the photograph.

"That was a hot LZ out there, but a lot of the VC just

seemed to disappear. Even with the casualties they've had we haven't seen enough for this size of base. I've got a feeling they're here, but we just can't see 'em. Most of the battalion is out sweeping the jungle."

"Did you find any tunnels?"

The question seemed to make the captain pause for a moment. "Some holes in the ground. Deep holes. I thought they were just deep foxholes. Do you think they're down there?"

Sanders merely glanced at the American adviser.

"Okay, we'll blow up the holes. That should give 'em something to think about."

Sanders nodded toward the wall. "Better take the map."

The captain ripped it down, and McWaters handed him the stack of papers as he walked out.

"Lazar was here?" asked McWaters. It was hot inside the bunker. His fatigue shirt was almost black with sweat, and his hair was plastered down on his forehead. The navy lieutenant looked around the bare room, expecting somehow to see something unique, an assassin's wardrobe or an array of weapons.

"This is where he hung out."

Sanders slipped the photo case into his shirt pocket. "Looks like we've done all we can here. We've wiped out a VC headquarters. MACV is going to be happy as hell."

They walked outside. Choppers were circling overhead, waiting to come down. ARVNs were leading a small group of prisoners back to the LZ. The VC had their arms bound behind them.

"Tell them to hold up a minute."

Chu called out and the Vietnamese soldiers stopped.

Sanders walked up to the prisoners. They were the usual boyish-looking peasants. One was a woman, probably a nurse, wearing a black-and-white checkered scarf. She stared back at him sullenly.

"Chu, bring her over here."

"Now wait a minute," McWaters exploded. "You're not going to do stuff like that to a woman."

Sanders smiled patiently at him. "Don't worry, bleeding heart. I'm just going to talk to her."

McWaters watched with anger and disgust as Chu and Le hustled the nurse over to the bunker. She stood between them, tiny like a child.

The ARVNs watched curiously. The American captain walked past with a group of Vietnamese officers, saw what they were doing, and kept going, head down.

"Chu," said Sanders. "Explain to her that we want to ask her one question." Chu spoke rapidly. "Tell her that if she answers it correctly, we'll see that she is protected from the ARVNs. She won't be sent to the ARVN prison camp. Tell her that if she goes to a prison camp, she'll probably not come out alive. Tell her that the guards will rape her every day. She will be tortured. She will eat filth. She will live in the camp for years, covered with sores and dirt, until she dies. If she helps us, she will go to an American prison. She will eat good food and be well-treated. One day she'll be quietly released and can return to her village. No one will know."

Chu chattered on. When he finished he slapped the woman hard across the face to get the point across.

"Chu," said Sanders quietly.

The woman hung between the two Vietnamese, hair falling across her face. Flies buzzed around her head. The sun seemed to beat down like a sledgehammer. One of the ARVNs called something, and the Vietnamese laughed. Le made a gesture to them, and they all laughed again.

Sanders spoke quietly. "Ask her where is her commissar. Commissar La-zar."

The nurse said nothing for a moment. She stared up at Sanders through strands of her hair with hate and loathing that was almost tangible.

"Let me hit, Major," said Chu. He swung back his hand.

"Chu, take out your knife." The Vietnamese grinned and pulled his bayonet knife out of its scabbard. McWaters started forward but stopped when Sanders looked at him with eyes like ice. Suddenly the woman started to talk. Her face was down and you had to strain to hear her.

"She say La-zar was here. But he did not come back after, ah, attack on American post at A Shau. She think he is dead." The woman fell silent.

Sanders looked at her for a moment, sweat trickling down his rugged features, then nodded. "Okay, keep her with us until we get back. We'll turn her over to the MPs at Bien Hoa." McWaters seemed to breathe easier. Chu waved the ARVNs on, and they walked off, jeering and laughing at the Americans, pulling the wretched group of captured VC.

Off in the jungle there was a series of explosions, then a very big bang. Hot dirt showered down on them, and the ground shook. Black smoke drifted above the treetops. The ARVNs were pulling back to the landing zone. Two ARVN sappers ran past with explosives to blow up the kitchens.

"Do you think he's dead?"

"I doubt it," Sanders mused, staring off into the distance. "The Lazar I know is a survivor. But he's screwed up badly. Now he has to redeem himself. No, old Jai's holed up somewhere, waiting for an opportunity. Thing is, he may already have one picked out."

They started to hike back to the LZ between knots of ARVNs, chattering and boasting, the nurse cowering between Chu and Le. Le had tied her to him with a length of heavy cord. Sentries stood off in the bushes, alert in case of a VC counterattack.

"Would you really have let Chu use his knife on her?" McWaters stared anxiously at the craggy-faced man walking next to him. Sanders seemed to be breathing hard, as if he had just been running. His shirt was soaked with sweat across his shoulders and down his chest and back.

"Hell, Davey, you know me. Would I do something like that?" Sanders laughed loudly and walked on. But McWaters followed him with a sudden feeling of resolve. The decision had been made. He knew he was leaving Vietnam—in fact, he was leaving the navy. He'd finished his required service, anyway. What they were doing was perhaps necessary—even that was arguable—but one thing he was absolutely sure of was the fact that it was not meant for him. From now on, he counted the days.

14

THE DEAN OF the diplomatic corps in any city is supposed to be the diplomat or consul of longest residence or most senior standing. But diplomats represent the power of their respective countries, and, consequently, social functions at the residences and embassies of the most powerful inevitably carry the greatest cachet among those who pride themselves, as a professional matter, on believing the term "realist" represents the highest of accolades. As the fortunes of nations rise or decline in the affairs of the world—especially in regard to how many battalions they can field or, in the case of the twentieth century, the strength of their claim to being a nuclear power—so, too, does the prestige of their embassies. It is not surprising then that an invitation to a reception at the American ambassador's Residence, no matter how long it had been since the ambassador presented his credentials to the head of state, was the paramount event on the social calendar of the diplomatic corps in Saigon. That evening the lower floor of the Residence was crowded with guests—a glittering and beribboned cross-section of diplomats and staff from a dozen embassies, soldiers, businessmen, artists, and politicians. Smiling with professional ease, they talked shop, traded the latest gossip, noted who was present and who was not, and remembered to take a drink from one of the waiters who unobtrusively glided around the room with practiced skill.

Margaret Vossenack, standing in a group with Robert,

the U.S. Embassy's deputy protocol officer, and a crewcut young assistant air attache, glanced around the room to make sure all was proceeding smoothly. Her practiced eye noted the supply of food on the buffet, the quantity of champagne being consumed, and carefully noted who was ensconced in a corner with whom.

She saw that the Turkish ambassador, reputed to have a pornography collection of legendary proportions, had managed to trap a young secretary from the British embassy between an armoir and the back of an Australian colonel. In another corner, a Japanese businessman was deep in conversation with two Vietnamese generals—she idly wondered what unimaginable deal was being cooked up there—while loud laughter erupted from the spot where Bud Bailey was describing a football game, the season's clincher, to several middle-aged American Army advisers from MACV.

Robert was telling the latest gossip. A group of intellectuals had tried to hold a press conference in a restaurant in the center of Saigon. They were presenting a petition to the government. Vietnamese Special Forces troops had arrived and arrested everybody, including the newspaper people who were present. Vossenack had had to personally protest to the Minister of Information before the correspondents of the *New York Times* and *Newsweek* were released.

"—not that a stay in jail would do them any harm," the ambassador was saying. Then he stared. "Good lord, who invited him?"

Margaret glanced over to the door in time to see Lewis Sanders walk in. For a moment she felt her face going red. Dimly, she remembered telling the embassy protocol officer to add Sanders's name to the reception list some weeks ago but had then forgotten to tell her to remove it after the ordeal at Sanders's hotel.

"I'm afraid I must plead guilty, dear."

They all eyed Sanders with interest as he picked up a drink from a passing waiter.

"Well at least he's cleaned himself up a little," said Vossenack. Sanders had managed to have his tan suit cleaned and pressed and was wearing a clean white shirt and a dark necktie. He even seemed to have made an attempt to comb his hair.

"Oh, Mr. Ambassador, that's unkind. Mr. Sanders seems such a nice man to me," said the deputy protocol officer. "I met him in the officers' club at MACV the other day and he was so gracious." She was a large dark-haired woman from New Orleans with a Scarlet O'Hara accent. Margaret looked at her with new interest.

"I hear that Major Sanders is not one to stand on ceremony," grinned the assistant air attache. "Did you hear that he got into an argument with Colonel Mooney at MACV over the organization of the South Vietnamese Army? They ended up shouting at each other."

"That sounds like Sanders," said Vossenack grimly.

"I understand, though, that he's been somewhat successful. In his work here, I mean," the young Air Force officer spoke guardedly but stopped when he received an icy look from Vossenack.

"I wouldn't say that what could be called his success is due to his actions alone," said Vossenack stiffly. "Young Lieutenant McWaters over there is bird-dogging our major. Now there's a bright young officer—should go far in the service."

"Well, I guess you can't expect that much from someone who's been out of things for a while. Sanders is old enough to have been in World War Two," said the assistant air attache, trying to cover his mistake with a joke.

"Captain, I happen to be old enough to have been in World War Two," said Vossenack, glaring at the hapless airman. Margaret had trouble hiding her smile.

141

David McWaters, wearing a pressed summer khaki uniform and holding a canape in one hand and a glass in the other, almost bumped into someone as he backed away from a crowd around a waiter. "Oh, I'm very sorry," he said, trying to keep his hand steady and then he stopped and stared. She was a young Vietnamese and the most beautiful woman he had ever seen. For a moment he could do nothing but gaze at her shiny raven hair falling in soft waves around a perfectly formed face. She wore a traditional *ao dais* of light blue silk that shimmered in the light.

"I'm sorry for staring. I was just wondering what I was going to say to St. Peter," he said.

"St. Peter?" she looked puzzled.

"Why yes, I must be in heaven."

She laughed, white even teeth showing between ruby lips.

"My name is David McWaters."

"My name is Vo Thi Yen. But that's my Vietnamese name. I am also called Anna Vo." Her voice was soft and melodious, only the trace of an accent.

"Well, Anna Vo, you must do something important that deserves two names?"

She smiled, "I am an actress."

"Really? The Vietnamese stage or in films."

"I began on the stage, but I mostly act in films now. Some of them Vietnamese films, some in other parts of Asia. I have just returned from Hong Kong. I had a small role in a film there."

"Ah, should I see it?"

"I am afraid it will not be very good. It is about kung fu. I am a princess who is rescued by a brave kung fu expert who . . ." she searched for a word, "destroys three hundred bad men to rescue me."

They both laughed.

"We make a lot of films like that in the United States.

They're called Westerns. Have you ever been to Hollywood, Miss Vo?"

"Please, call me Anna. No, I haven't. But perhaps one day I will make a film there. It is one of my ambitions."

"Can I get you a drink, Anna," he said.

"Please, I will have some champagne."

McWaters dived through the crowd to find a waiter. The room was becoming crowded. He glimpsed Sanders in conversation with an Australian officer. The burly man saw him and nodded. The navy lieutenant came back with a glass of champagne and found a New Zealand Army captain talking to Anna. The captain smiled awkwardly and edged away when McWaters stared hard at him.

"Have you seen much of Saigon since you have been here, Mr. McWaters?"

"If you're Anna then I'm Dave, although some people call me Davey. Well, I've seen quite a bit of the city. It's a fascinating place. But I must admit, I see a lot that I don't understand. Vietnam is somewhat a mystery to me. I think it's that way to most Westerners. I hope you don't mind my saying this," he added anxiously.

"No, I understand. Vietnam is very unique. It is a very old country, and perhaps only a Vietnamese can really understand it. The French could never understand Vietnam, although I don't think they really wanted to. They valued their own culture so much more."

"I must admit my knowledge of Vietnam begins with the French." Sanders looked down into the deep brown eyes of the actress. I have never seen anyone so beautiful, he thought. Her hair had a deep sheen like a raven's wing. Above her eyebrow, a faint scar.

She seemed to acknowledge his intense gaze and smiled. "But there's so much more to Vietnamese history," she pretended to be scolding. "Vietnam was once part of the Chinese Empire—for over a thousand years.

Then the Vietnam people rebelled and fought for their freedom. The war with China went on for centuries. In 39 A.D., according to your Western calendar, the revolt was led by the Trung sisters. They are great patriots of Vietnam. My country finally gained its independence from China in the tenth century."

McWaters was fascinated.

"I had no idea. Were there any revolts against the French?"

"Oh, yes. They began in the nineteen-twenties. One revolutionary group was in the north, in the—ah, delta?—delta of the Red River. It was called the VNQDD. I won't spell out the Vietnamese name for you. It was a group of patriots from all, what do you say? all walks of life. The French killed them all and bombed their villages. It was very sad."

"Were the rebels Communists?"

"No, not Communists. They were patriots who wanted a free Vietnam. That is the tragedy of my country. Now the choices are so limited."

He felt embarrassed for a moment. As if, as a Westerner, he was partially responsible for the problems of Vietnam. "I hope you can tell me more about your country, Anna. I have a lot to learn."

Sanders found himself alone in the room. For the third time he wondered why he had come. He was not comfortable at functions like this. Not that he felt out of his depth. He just had never liked cocktail parties, even if this one was dressed up in diplomatic regalia. Across the room, he saw McWaters deep in conversation with a stunning young Vietnamese woman. Margaret Vossenack drifted into his vision for a moment. They had so far managed to avoid each other. Her pale green dress seemed to complement her blond hair, which had been arranged down on either side of her face to touch the gold necklace that set off the pale skin of her neck. Sanders stared moodily down into his drink.

"A long way from California."

Sanders looked up and saw Felix Corman. He was startled for a moment and then broke into a wide grin.

"Felix, what the hell. You do something wrong, too?"

Felix grinned back. "Probably," he said in a low voice. "They've just sent me out to run the shop here."

"Well, that's something. Station Chief. I should give you my congratulations, but I'll think I'll wait until you've been here a while. You may not want them."

"I hear it's getting hairy."

"Some."

Corman went on talking quietly. "I also hear that you're getting close to our friend with the gun. Come around to the office. Early tomorrow. We'll talk."

Sanders nodded. "Well, I'm glad you're here anyway, Felix, and I hope you've got a direct channel to whoever it is pulls the strings back there in Langley. We need some real life out here."

Felix nodded. "We'll talk, Lew." He wandered off into the crowd.

Sanders began to make his way across the room toward the buffet. As he pushed through the crowd, he suddenly came face to face with the Vossenacks.

"Good evening, Major," said Vossenack stiffly.

"Mr. Ambassador. How are you, Mrs. Vossenack?"

"Fine, thank you, Major Sanders." She seemed to look over his shoulder. Her voice was icy.

"I've been hearing some good things about your project here, Sanders," said Vossenack. There was grudging recognition in his voice.

"Lucky, I guess. But there's something I think you should know, Mr. Ambassador. I think there's a leak somewhere in the embassy. Someone's passing out information. Probably a Vietnamese."

"Well, I'll get the embassy security team to look into it. But we can hardly do without our Vietnamese employees. It would just not be practical."

"Thought I'd mention it, Mr. Ambassador." Sanders nodded and moved on.

Margaret's eyes followed him as he worked his way through the crowd. She barely heard her husband saying something. Another burst of laughter erupted from the group around Bud Bailey. There was a sudden stir in the crowded room and Ngo Dinh Nhu walked in with an entourage of bodyguards and aides. He was wearing a well-cut gray Western suit. As he nodded and smiled at the guests, Robert guided Margaret forward to greet him.

"Best behavior, Margaret," he murmured. "Let's meet the second most important man in the country."

Sanders watched the flurry as Nhu entered the room.

"I hear his wife is the real power behind the throne," said the Australian colonel.

"Oh, she can't be as bad as they say," said the British secretary.

"Women, young lady, always have the greatest power," said the Turkish ambassador, almost sadly.

The reception eddied and swirled around Nhu as the diplomats came forward to pay their respects. Vietnamese generals smiled and edged closer to the man who guided their nation. Sanders wandered around the room. He was introduced to Anna Vo by McWaters, said something complimentary, and moved on. Suddenly off in the distance there was a tremendous explosion, and the windows were lit by a flash, rattling as a shock wave hit the building. Conversation stopped, and then resumed nervously. Nhu's bodyguards clustered about him tightly as he prepared to leave. Distant sirens wailed. Vossenack and General Bachelor hurried over to say a few words to him.

"Bombs bursting in air," said a voice behind Margaret. She turned; it was Lewis Sanders.

"I don't really think we have anything to say to each other, Major Sanders."

"Look, I guess I owe you an apology. I'm sorry. I had things figured wrong."

She hesitated. "Accepted. We'll forget the whole thing."

"Can I make amends by getting you a drink?"

She noticed he was still wearing his scuffed cowboy boots. "Yes, but I've been meaning to ask you. Why are you staying in that dreadful place?"

"The Great Asia? Lee Chung runs a tight ship. And I get free *dim sum* from the restaurant downstairs."

They both laughed.

Outside, police cars and trucks roared past the embassy. Sirens continued their jarring wail, and flames from a burning building flickered in the distance.

"I wonder how long this will go on," said Margaret, staring out through the window.

"Until someone wins," replied Sanders.

Much later that evening, as they prepared for bed, Margaret casually brought up the subject of the strange Major Sanders. Her husband was lying on the bed reading some papers and seemed irritated by the question.

"Sanders? Yes, a man with little discipline and even less staying power. I understand he now sells building lots to rich Californians. It's probably just one of the jobs he's done."

"You don't seem to like him much, Robert."

"Can't say that I do. He was attached to my division temporarily in Korea. Not temporarily enough as far as I was concerned." Vossenack shuffled the papers in irritation. Then he put them aside and stared across the room. "Sanders blames me for the loss of a lot of his men in his company. When the Red Chinese entered the war all hell broke loose, and it was a very confused situation for a time. Sanders's ranger company had been pretty badly mauled, and he was trying to get his men back across a bridge to safety. We were ordered by Corps to pull back to form another line. An ROK division had fallen apart on our flank, and we had no choice. We blew the bridge because if we hadn't the Red Chinese would have gotten across it. But that left the rangers on the other side. They had to fight their way across some mountains to link up with a marine division. Sanders was badly wounded, and he lost a lot more of his men."

"Well surely he knows it was not your fault."

"It wasn't the decision to pull back that bugs him. All that's written in the official history for anyone to read. He thinks we could have delayed blowing the bridge until his company got across." Vossenack seemed to be seeing another time and place. "It was a decision I had to make. I just didn't know how close the Reds were. I couldn't jeopardize the division, maybe even the corps." He paused for a moment, staring at the wall, seeing something. Margaret waited for him to go on.

"But the fact remains," Vossenack finally continued, "that Sanders just doesn't like to take orders. He felt then that he knew better than his superiors, and he still feels that way. You just can't have someone like that in the chain-of-command, where so much depends on teamwork and knowing that you can depend on someone to get the job done. He just wasn't a good officer."

"Yet he seems to have a certain ability in more— perhaps unconventional situations."

"Oh, I'll grant you that. Sanders is a lone wolf, and I guess there's a place for a loner once in a while—as long as he recognizes that he's not playing his own game out there. The trouble with his kind of individual is that, ultimately, you just can't trust them." With a final look of annoyance at Margaret, Vossenack picked up his papers and continued reading them.

Margaret brushed her hair, regarding herself in the mirror of her dressing table. Perhaps Sanders has a clearer view of what's wrong with the rules of the game, she thought. Sometimes you have to make the rules fit the game and not the other way around.

15

THE PROSTITUTE'S APARTMENT consisted of one room in a shabby building near the Saigon docks. It was a neighborhood of warehouses, cafés, and brothels that looked out on garbage-strewn alleys puddled with diesel fuel and rainwater and filled with the stench of rotten fish and gasoline. In its crowded streets, filled with poverty-stricken refugees from the countryside, where gangs of children stole to stay alive, the bribe was a way of life and no one knew who was worse—the drug dealers and black marketeers or the police who ruled the area like an independent fiefdom.

There is a story that the Saigon police were once sold to the Binh Xuyen religious cult by Emperor Bao Dai, supposedly to pay his gambling debts. Under its leader, Bay Vien, a brigadier general in the Vietnamese National Army, the Binh Xuyen also ran Saigon's largest gambling casino, the Grande Monde, which included the "Hall of Mirrors," a brothel with twelve hundred women. Diem crushed the Binh Xuyen's private army in 1955, and its remnants retreated to the Mekong Delta. Eventually, the Binh Xuyen troops, along with the private armies of the Cao Dai and the Hoa Hao religious sects, joined the NLF in its fight against the Saigon government.

The sound of horns from the ships on the river penetrated the prostitute's tiny apartment. She had cut photographs from newspapers and magazines, Asian film stars and entertainers, and stuck them on the wall above the bed. A beaded curtain separated the kitchen from the single room. The prostitute was twenty years old, a country girl from a rural province, blank faced and pretty, her straight hair cut in a fringe across her forehead. Her husband had been killed in an ARVN sweep the year before. They had accused the village of sheltering VC and picked out five men to shoot as an example. Her husband had been one of the examples, and the crash of the rifle fire that ended his life would echo in her mind forever. With the death of her husband, her choices had been few. She had drifted into the city carrying her child in a swollen belly. After its birth, it had been prostitution or slow starvation. For six months she had been an opium addict.

Lazar sat at the rickety table, the room lit by a bare lightbulb, and watched her nurse the sickly child. The leader of the local Peoples Liberation Front cell had recruited her. In the new society, there would be no prostitution, he had told her. But she seemed little interested in revolutionary ideals. It was her burning hatred of the Diem government that committed her to the cause; revenge for her husband's death, the motivator.

There was something wrong with the baby. Anyone could see that. It was wasting away, staring up at her with huge eyes as she cooed at it hour after hour, keeping to itself a secret of immeasurable depth.

As Lazar watched the woman he thought of his wife. They had divorced years ago. She had been a Catholic from a prominent family in Hue, their marriage arranged by their parents—unusual for Vietnam, where women had always been more emancipated than any other country in Asia. He had been twenty-one, she nineteen. There had been a certain amount of reluctance on the part of the bride's side of the pact. After all, he was of mixed blood. But Lazar's father had been a rising official in the colonial government, an important contact for a family of merchants. Besides, they had other daughters.

Now he could hardly remember what she looked like. A quiet doll-like girl. Did they ever have a single conversation? What she would have preferred to have done was to study pharmacy, a position of prestige and importance. When he went into the jungle to fight the Japanese, they had said good-bye awkwardly, as if it were between strangers. Later he had written to her about his acceptance of communism, urging her to read this book, that pamphlet. There had been no answer, and some months later he had heard from his father. His wife was divorcing him.

A gentle tap at the door. The young prostitute answered it, carrying the child on one arm. It was a teenage boy, sidling into the room and standing by the door, staring at Lazar. There were a few he could trust to obey his orders. A few here in Saigon and in the village.

"Here is the message. It goes to the American, Sanders. Only he must see it. You understand? And this message goes to comrade Lanh at Ben Thong."

The boy nodded. He tucked the scraps of paper in the pocket of his white shirt, whispered something to Lazar, and left quickly. There was a mournful hoot from the river. The girl sang softly to her baby. Lazar said a few words to the girl. She put down the child carefully on the bed and went to the wardrobe. From the bottom, a pile of plastic bags and rolled clothing, she took a small bundle wrapped in a rag. She watched Lazar blankly as he unwrapped it. It was a Polish K-54 pistol and a box of shells. As he fed the small cartridges into the clip, she began to coo again to the silent baby.

The police colonel was eating noisily, his jacket open, showing a bulging stomach. He was always a greedy man. The Chinese merchant, ascetically sparse, sat across the table from him, amused by the gluttony.

"What do you hear?" said the colonel.

The merchant's coal black eyes gleamed. He picked carefully at the vegetables on the plate before him with his chopsticks.

"There is a rumor that the Americans no longer trust Diem. The generals seem to gather here and there."

The police colonel belched. "I know that, Chan. Everyone knows that. But is there a time, a date?"

The Chinese merchant was impassive. The police colonel's wife was also a greedy woman. He had handled many illegal currency transactions for her. He knew the colonel was worried, concerned with how much the merchant knew about his family's activities. It gave him a certain power. The colonel was nervous, careful not to offend.

"Perhaps your American friends . . ."

The colonel snorted. "The Americans pay well, which they are wise to do because they rely on us for their information."

The merchant looked at the other man eating, gobbling the food as if any second someone would take it away. The Lao Tzu said there is no calamity greater than lavish desires and no greater disaster than greed. Strange that he should live this way, in this city of turmoil, and still believe in Tao. An accident of birth. A father who chose to leave his native Canton to make money in Saigon instead of in Singapore or San Francisco. Many things would happen in this city before it found peace. The Lao Tzu also said that if the earth has not become tranquil, it will soon be shaken. Saigon will shake, and many will fall. And he? He moved with the tide, honored his father, believed in Tao—and worked with the Communists.

Through the beaded curtain that separated their booth from the rest of the restaurant the merchant could see it was almost empty. He felt a draft, a gust of cool air, as a door was opened. Across from him, the colonel went on eating, oblivious.

"There are more rumors," said Chan. Then, almost casually. "They say Minh might be involved."

The colonel looked up quickly. That was news. If Minh was involved . . . He stared blankly at the Chinese. A worm of panic squirmed in his stomach. Perhaps it was time to not count too heavily on the patronage of Nhu. Perhaps he should be building bridges elsewhere. He gulped, his chopsticks nervously searching for the last morsel in his bowl.

"What are our friends in the woods up to?"

The Chinese smiled. "They gain strength."

"They did not seem to do very well in that attack on the American hill base."

A footstep near the booth. The merchant leaned toward the curtain, shifting his weight.

"They are displeased."

The colonel looked up again, wide-eyed, fear on his face.

"The information you passed along about the hill base. You did not mention the special artillery the Americans had. It was responsible for the death of many of our friends."

"I knew nothing about that," the colonel gasped. "I do not know what weapons they would have there from week to week."

"Also," said the Chinese, as if he had not heard, "it is said that you have been seeing a lot of known CIA agents. You admit that they pay you well. And you have also been asking questions about a certain individual. A commissar of the NLF battalion that was severely beaten at the hill base. A man who also does special work in the city. Our friends feel that you have been dealing with too many sides, my colonel."

Shadows moved on the other side of the bead curtain. The police colonel stared at them as if paralyzed. He seemed to choke as the curtain was pushed back. Two men stood there. An older man, hard-looking, dressed in black, and a younger man who stood slightly behind him. The Chinese merchant dived out of the booth and was gone in an instant as the older man leveled an automatic pistol. The police colonel whimpered in terror, trying to stand in the confined space, his mouth opening and closing, bowls overturning. The sound of the three shots came quickly, almost as one, and the colonel collapsed in the narrow seat, blood on the front of his white suit. The two assassins quickly left the restaurant. One of the cooks, hearing the noise, came out of the kitchen. He gaped after them, open-mouthed, and then went to the booth. The police colonel was lying on the floor. He was still clutching an empty bowl. The other hand was dug into a cushion, as if it could save him.

There were footsteps behind him. It was the Chinese merchant with two other men. A curt command. The cook shrank back and retreated into the kitchen. They were big men, known gangsters. Later, he peered cautiously out into the restaurant again. The body had gone.

When Lazar knocked on the door she let him in, and then sat on the bed watching him. The baby was asleep, lying on a folded sheet in an open box. Lazar slid the gun under a pillow, then drank a bottle of warm beer, his mouth dry with thirst. The girl still stared at him as if waiting for some signal or a sign that would make all things clear. Something that could explain the death of a husband, a life of misery, a dying child. Later, he made love to her, sweating in the darkness, senses alert for a false sound, a footfall.

"We should not move yet. There is time to catch them all." The mandarin carefully quartered the orange.

"That's nonsense. It may be too late." His brother, the president, glanced nervously around the room, his voice dropping to a hiss as a servant entered to clear away dishes from the table where they had just eaten. Diem sat in a brocaded armchair, brushing nervously at ashes on the knee of his white suit, holding his cigarette high so that the nicotine would not stain his fingers.

"Why leave rot in the fruit? It's better to catch them all. They will eventually betray themselves. It will give us an excuse to deal harshly with them. The Americans can understand that. If we simply imprison them now, move them to overseas posts, it will just create the impression of more instability and our indecision."

The president smoked his cigarette, inhaling deeply. He was overwrought, tired. He could see the logic, but his brother did not seem to understand the fine edge on which he governed. They had let things deteriorate too much. It was not his brother who had to continually stall the American ambassador. "We must do something about the Buddhists, Nhu. It's time for an accommodation. I don't think the Americans are going to be patient much longer. Their Voice of America broadcasts are blaming your police for the pagoda raids. They are absolving the army. It's not a good sign."

The mandarin, sitting at the table, sucked on a piece of the orange, letting the juice run into a napkin held under his chin. "We must consolidate our power. Make sure the generals are loyal to us. The Buddhists are helpless. What can they do? They set fire to themselves. It makes us look bad to the Americans. But we know that they are powerless."

Diem looked at his brother. He could never understand him. Even as children, it was Nhu who made the plans, who seemed to carry within him a burning zeal that swept them both along to some ultimate destiny that he could barely comprehend. And Nhu's wife, she seemed to know what they were thinking, anticipate every possible move. He sometimes had the impression that all of them—the family—seemed to be on the top of a volcano, and they could not move even a foot or a finger, otherwise it would destroy them.

"We have our contact with the generals," his brother went on. He sucked some more juice. "He will keep us informed."

The president sighed. "We'll wait then, but not too long."

"Perhaps," said his brother, wiping his fingers carefully, "we should move some of the Special Force into the Palace. As a precaution."

"Dangerous," said Felix. He was gazing out of his office window through a plastic shade, squinting in the early morning sunlight, watching a parade of Buddhist demonstrators. There were perhaps a hundred of them, walking in chanting rows. Pedestrians along the sidewalk watched the monks impassively. A sign said, "Get Out U.S.A." The parade was going toward the Presidential Palace, but Felix knew it would never reach it.

He had done little more to make the room habitable than had his predecessor, a few more books on the shelves, a more comfortable chair, a Chinese print on the wall. It must be some sort of personality trait that goes with the occupation, thought Sanders, a tendency for self-effacement, to reveal little about oneself. A direct contradiction to his vocation of trying to know all about everyone else. The police mentality, an overwhelming curiosity about other people's lives while remaining anonymous yourself. A sort of voyeur's profession. Or perhaps it was just the transient anonymity of a bureaucrat's office.

"I was expecting it. He must be getting desperate. The options are closing for him. He has no more maneuvering room."

"We could seal off the area. Swamp the whole place with cops."

"Lazar knows that rabbit warren like the back of his hand. And you know that security's terrible. He'll never show up."

"This is a police job, Lew. We should let the Surete handle it."

"Lazar will only talk to me."

"He's setting you up. He's going to try to kill you."

Sanders did not reply.

"Okay, hero, what do you suggest?"

Sanders spread his hands. "Do like the note says. He wants to talk. Maybe he's willing to come over. I'll take just my team—McWaters, Chu, and Le. The Four Musketeers."

"You believe that? He's willing to give himself up."

Sanders shrugged. "Worth a try."

Felix shook his head, uncertain. "You said you got the message as you were leaving your hotel this morning?"

"Yup, kid pushed it into my hand. He was gone before I could do anything."

"What did he look like?"

"Just a Vietnamese kid. Seventeen, maybe eighteen. Dressed like everyone else. A kid."

"It's dangerous for you to be living in that hotel down there. Move out of it. Take a room at BOQ, the Continental, out at Bien Hoa. Anywhere. But get out of that hotel. That's an order."

"Okay, Felix," said Sanders resignédly.

Felix sat down at his desk and looked at Sanders carefully, trying to catch a smile of deception, an insubordinate grin. But Sanders gazed back at him innocently.

"All right. You know your men and you know the situation. Have you got a handgun?"

"No."

"Here." Felix shoved across a .38 police special and

a leather holster. He dug around in the bottom drawer of his desk again and produced a belt-loop ammunition holder with about a dozen rounds. "You shouldn't need more than that. If you do, you've lost it, anyway. Tell your men they can pick up weapons from the marine armory downstairs." He scribbled something on a message slip and slid it across the desk. "Have them give the marine guard this."

Sanders smiled ruefully. He pocketed the ammunition and removed the pistol from its holster, which he left on the desk. He got up to leave, picking up Felix's authorization.

"And Lew."

Sanders paused, shoving the revolver into his pocket. Felix looked up at him and smiled.

"Nail the son of a bitch."

It was almost dark when the team's Renault taxi, an old machine with yellow and blue markings, approached the warehouse district. Crowds still thronged the sidewalks, clustering around the food stalls. Shops displayed colored lanterns. Firecrackers suddenly sputtered and popped down a sidestreet, and McWaters caught a glimpse of a fierce dragon shaking its head in the light from a street lamp. A crowd of schoolchildren watched.

"Mid-Autumn Festival," Chu murmured. A festival for children.

The taxi dropped them several blocks from the river, Sanders paying the previously agreed price. The taxi had no meter. It spun away, the driver looking fearfully over his shoulder. The four of them walked, strung out some yards apart, down a sidestreet toward a row of warehouses that fronted on a dock, separating it from the rest of the neighborhood. They could hear the sound of ships moving on the river beyond the tall metal-and-concrete buildings. Masts, dim now in the twilight, showed above the metal roofs.

Vietnam seemed to have an insatiable demand for cement, and the smell of it inside the warehouse was overpowering. Sanders played his flashlight over the stacked bags, like pale mountains reaching almost to the girders supporting the roof. There was an alleyway between the stacks running down the center of the building. Aisles jutted off on either side at regular intervals. McWaters, Chu, and Le moved into the building behind him, trying to move silently but their feet crunching in the loose cement dust.

They stopped in a group, silent, listening. A ship hooted from the river, moving out on the high tide. McWaters peered from the dusty window. It was now dark, but groups of pedestrians still wandered up the street. A battered neon sign flashed over a café door, and another Renault taxi coasted slowly past. They waited. The darkness inside the vast warehouse was relieved only by a single red lightbulb that glowed over a door down at the far end of the center aisle.

The minutes ticked by. A group of drunken Polish sailors staggered past, singing. Another ship hooted mournfully. Further along the waterfront, they could see arc lights where stevedores were working at another warehouse. A truck rumbled past.

Chu and Le squatted on the floor. McWaters paced slowly, trying to muffle a cough. Sanders waited, looking at his watch. A faint noise made everyone turn swiftly. Sanders switched on his flashlight, catching two eyes that shone back at him in the beam of light.

"Rat."

Le muttered something and threw a piece of wood. It thudded on the dusty floor. The animal disappeared instantly.

Another auto, a black Citroen, drove slowly past the

warehouse doorway. It turned into an alley at the end of the street.

"Could be him."

Sanders said nothing. A group of Vietnamese stevedores came out of the café and walked toward the wharf in noisy conversation. Someone slammed a window.

The noise to their left was faint, a creak of a door, a faint screech of metal or a footstep. Sanders motioned to the others then began to walk slowly down the center aisle, moving carefully on the balls of his feet. There was complete silence. Even the traffic outside seemed to have stopped. Another noise, still on his left. He switched the flashlight to his left hand and felt for the pistol. He came to an aisle and stopped. Suddenly he switched on the flashlight, his gun out, crouching. There was nothing, dust circled in the cone of light. He switched it off and moved forward again. He was conscious of a footstep behind him, knew that it was one of his men following closely.

A ship close by hooted suddenly, the noise like an explosion. It seemed to emphasize the silence in the cavernous building.

"Jai," Sanders called quietly. He glanced back. He could make out Chu behind him. He knew McWaters and Le were circling somewhere on his right.

"Jai." Still no sound. He moved on down the center aisle. A passageway on his left was empty. So was one on his right. He was shifting his weigh to his right foot to move forward again, when Chu shouted. A dark figure, almost a shadow. There was a shot, a terrific explosion in the metal building, but Sanders had already dropped. He fired, knowing he was going to miss. Chu was shouting something, running forward. Sanders rolled to one side, trying to see the target. In the beam of dusty light there was another flash, the noise of the shot rebounding. He thought he saw a movement, a dim figure that showed for an instant against the pale sacks. The overhead lights suddenly flooded on. McWaters raced up, gun in hand. Sanders pointed to the left, shouted, and without breaking stride was running down an aisle. He stopped, panting. A door screeched.

"Here." He ran toward the sound. As he burst from behind a stack of bags, he saw a door swing, a glimpse at the periphery of his vision. He fired and glass shattered. A shadow moved for an instant and then was gone. Sanders rushed through the door and found himself in a garbage-filled alley. More cement bags on pallets. He splashed through a large puddle. At the end of the alley was the street, loud music from an apartment, the sound of a truck being loaded further along the wharf. Several people came to a doorway and stared across the street at him. Someone called. In the other direction, an elderly woman backed away from him and hurried into a doorway, muttering as she looked over her shoulder. He realized he was still holding the pistol and shoved it into his pocket. McWaters ran up.

"Lew, you'd better come."

Chu was lying on his back in the cement dust, his eyes open, staring at Sanders. A trickle of blood oozed from his mouth. He had taken a hit high on the chest, above the heart. Blood was seeping across his white shirt.

"Le is trying to get an ambulance."

At the end of the aisle a policeman in a tan uniform appeared with an elderly civilian. They stopped when they saw the Westerners. The policeman called something in Vietnamese, then turned and ran out. The elderly man stood staring, his mouth open. Chu gasped and tried to say something. Sanders patted his hand. Le came back, pushing roughly past the old man. Another policeman followed him, yelling questions. Le ignored him. Then the warehouse was filled with police and shouting ambulance attendants, lifting Chu onto a stretcher.

Somewhere in the background, Felix appeared with a group of Americans and Vietnamese in civilian clothes. Hard-faced men who watched silently. Chu was carried out to an ambulance. He seemed to shudder, a gout of blood came from his mouth. He turned his head as if to find someone, saw Sanders, and stared at the American. He grimaced, almost a smile. Then he was still. An attendant listened with a stethoscope and shook his head. He pulled a sheet over the still form. Sanders watched with McWaters and Le close behind him. All three said nothing, staring at the ambulance as it edged its way through the crowd, lights flashing. Sanders was conscious that someone was asking questions, but he found himself with nothing to say, only a blurring in the eyes that was probably caused by the acrid stench of fuel oil from the river.

16

AT THE CLUB NAUTIQUE on the Saigon River, between Nguyen Hue Street and the Ben Nghe Canal, Sanders watched a cat stalk a large gray rat.

He took a swallow from his gin and tonic, sitting alone at a corner table, and watched as the white-and-brown cat gathered its rear legs under its body for the leap. The odds were on the rat. It was a big, mean-looking thing. It looked up at Sanders for a moment as it held a piece of bread in its paws, its beady eyes staring unblinkingly at the major, nose twitching, as if it wanted to share some kind of secret that only they could appreciate. I know, the rat seemed to say, there is always something in life that wants to trap you. Only if you avoid the predictable can you stay free.

The cat sprang but the rat had the bread in its mouth and was already moving. The cat slammed into a chair, recovered, and dived after the rat. They both disappeared through a doorway into the kitchen. A white-coated waiter ignored the commotion as he carried out a loaded tray. There were only a few diners in the Club, some French expatriates, still unwilling to return to a cold and inhospitable France, two noisy Australians telling tall stories over "Thirty-Three" beer, a sprinkling of Vietnamese businessmen and their wives. Sanders lit a cigarette. He was about to order another drink when he spotted Margaret Vossenack standing uncertainly in the doorway.

He waved, standing up, and she came over, smiling.

She was wearing a white cotton print dress. Her blond hair swept down to the sides of her face. A thin rope of pearls gleamed dully on her white skin.

"I'm supposed to say, sorry, it was the traffic, but the fact is I started out late."

He grinned. "And I'm supposed to say I just got here myself. Can I get you a drink?"

She ordered a Tom Collins, and chattered on about social life at the embassy. The ambassador was in Guam for a conference with the Commander-in-Chief, Pacific and the Secretary of Defense. He listened, but it gave him little understanding of the intricate motions of government and diplomacy, another world from the bare brown hills of California.

"I hear that one of your men was killed."

He nodded, turning his lighter over in his hands.

"Yup. Chu, an ARVN soldier."

"You couldn't have known him long."

"No, not long."

She reached forward suddenly and held his hand, startling him by her touch. "Why do you do this?"

"That's funny. Someone else asked me that recently." He smiled quizzically at her. "I don't really know why I do this. I'm a soldier. It's something I do well."

"But you were in World War Two, and then Korea. You're not a professional. Surely that's enough."

"You've been finding out about me, Margaret."

She almost blushed, then laughed.

"Do you like being an ambassador's wife?"

"Usually. Like you, I do what I have to do rather well. But sometimes it's a routine." She paused. "Robert is a brilliant man. He's come a long way from where he started. He's bound to get even more important posts after his tour here. I—I have a son in West Point."

There was a roar of laughter from the drunken Australians; a Vietnamese couple, she noticed, looked at them with disgust.

"You must have been in Vietnam before, Lew. Was it during World War Two?"

He nodded. "I was with the OSS in the north, leading what we called a 'Mercy Team.' We were sent to coordinate things with the French and the Vietnamese resistance, try and establish some sort of order in the country after the Japanese surrender. It didn't work."

"Too many cooks?"

"Something like that. Everyone had different aims. The French wanted things to go back to where they were before the war. That was a little unrealistic. We wanted to get an independent, westward-oriented, democratic country with kids playing Little League. Maybe that was unrealistic, too. There was the Chinese Army in the north looting everything it could get its hands on, the British in Saigon trying to keep the natives in their place. And then there was Ho Chi Minh and the Communists, who had their own intentions, of course."

She shook her head sadly. "Dumb world. I sometimes—well, I sometimes wish my son had decided on something different than a military career." Then she was embarrassed because she suddenly remembered he was a soldier.

"I'm sorry, Lew."

"No, I understand."

Sanders looked at her steadily, noticing the way her hair curled onto her neck.

"Margaret," he said. "How's my timing this time?"

She gazed down at her drink for a moment. "I would say," she paused and looked up at him frankly, "I would say that your timing is very good."

"There's a town on the beach near here. Nha Trang," he said. "Would you like to come with me?"

She looked into his eyes searchingly. Then nodded, with an open smile.

He drove there in a rented Renault. Nha Trang was a beautiful little resort town built by the French. Small villas clustered around secluded courtyards, a clean beach spotted with striped umbrellas.

They rented a room in an old French-style hotel and that night she undressed self-consciously and got into bed quickly. Sanders seemed to throw off his clothes without a second look, and the bed sagged under his weight. Margaret tried to stop her mind as he kissed her, caressing her breasts, then parted her legs and moved into her. She seemed to be overcome by weariness, and afterward she lay in his arms tiredly. Consenting adulterers, she thought. But, when he began to caress her again, she stiffened, her body unyielding. An angry response almost burst from Sanders, but he stifled it. Rolling over, the thick trunk of his body massive and tanned, he picked a cigarette out of a packet on the nightstand.

"It's not going to work, is it?"

She shook her head, tears running down her face.

In the morning, they drove back to Saigon, hardly speaking. When he dropped her off some blocks from the Residence, she paused for an instance and touched his rugged, pockmarked face with her hand, looking at him with calm, serious eyes.

"Good-bye Lewis," she said. "I hope—" she stopped, and then she was gone.

Sanders watched her walk away along the sidewalk. A bright, fashionable woman.

Camera bulbs popped and flashed. Reporters pressed closer, some held up microphones. What was Anna's favorite food? Did she like working in Hong Kong? A Japanese reporter wanted to know if she had marriage plans. The reporter's face was deadly serious, intent on her answers. Did she have a suitor? Anna giggled and shook her head. Asian stars were expected to lead lives of sedate conformity. Her press agent leaned forward and said something in her ear. She giggled again and caught McWater's eye above the heads of the reporters. He grinned at her, enjoying the way she fielded the questions and the fun of watching the press jostle for position.

He had been given a few days to fly to Hong Kong to meet his father, who was in the city on business. It helped that his father, a prosperous manufacturer, dealt with an important New York law firm with Agency connections. By coincidence, Anna had a press conference in Hong Kong to coincide with the opening of her latest film, and they had taken the same flight.

The press agent was waving his hands, the reporters still firing questions. Finally, they began to file out of the conference room, laughing, putting away their cameras and notebooks, Anna becoming suddenly no more now than any other aspect of their jobs, like a typewriter or a drink in an air-conditioned bar.

Anna walked over to McWaters and introduced her press agent, Maury Felice, a slim Eurasian who spoke English with a Spanish accent. McWaters liked him immediately. The press agent had a friendly grin and seemed to like his work, which he took seriously but not so seriously that it wasn't fun. McWaters asked him to come along to lunch. They were meeting his father at the Hilton. But Felice begged off.

"You two enjoy yourselves. But Anna, nothing I have to explain later," he said with mock seriousness. He shoved some eight-by-ten glossies into his briefcase. "I've got to run." He gave Anna a peck on the cheek. " 'Bye, dear, I'll call you in a few days. The deal with Rim Shan looks good." He shook hands again with the lieutenant and then hurried quickly out the door.

"Busy man."

"Oh yes. Maury is good at his work, and he's much in demand by actors like me. I'm lucky to get him."

They strolled along the packed sidewalk toward the hotel where his father was staying, the newish Mandarin on Connaught Road. The streets seemed jammed, Mercedes Benzes and double-decker trolleys cheek-by-jowl with small Japanese trucks and Australian-made sedans. Everywhere there were signs, banners, and street stalls, workers crammed into tiny offices above tiny stores. As they walked along, people stared at the attractive couple, and McWaters had the feeling that this attention was not what a CIA man should be receiving, but he grinned and enjoyed it anyway.

McWaters's father rose to meet them as they were shown to his table in the Grill, and he shook hands with Anna in frank admiration and said something jovial about wishing he'd had the advantages of the modern navy when he was in the service. Richard McWaters had inherited a small furniture manufacturing company from his father and built it into a big furniture manufacturing company, now branching into specialized office furniture and office "systems." He was a tall, gray-haired man with a genial frank expression and gray eyes that regarded you appraisingly from behind rimless eyeglasses; his passions were his family, his business, and collecting American Primitive art and books on the American Civil War. In that order.

Lunch passed in pleasant chitchat, and then they spent part of the afternoon sight-seeing, taking a tram up to the Peak, before Anna had to leave for an appointment with a film director. Over drinks at the Harlequin Bar with a view of the harbor, father and son regarded each other. David seemed different to his father. The last few months seemed to have changed him. The young man was gaunter somehow, lines etched around his eyes that his father had never noticed before. And yet he seemed stronger, tougher, a man who knew how to handle himself if he had to. He was also more serious, a reserve that was new.

"Feeling all right, Davey?" Richard McWaters contemplated his son carefully. Hong Kong Harbor was spread out before them. In the distance, Kowloon and the New Territories; beyond, the hills of China. All types of crafts puttered around the harbor—large freighters, junks, sampans, the gray bulk of a giant American aircraft carrier, dwarfing a flotilla of smaller ships that clustered around it.

"Fine, Dad. I take it Mom and Patty are okay?"

Yes, his mother was fine and his sister, in pre-Med at Cornell, was doing well.

"You seem tired, David. Things tough in Vietnam?"

"They keep me busy."

Richard McWaters nodded. He knew that his son, attached to the CIA, probably couldn't talk about what he was doing, nor did he expect him to.

"Are you—er, serious with Anna, Dave? Or is it just one of those things?" He grinned.

"You mean a girl in every port?"

"Well . . ." His father made a noncommittal gesture.

"Oh, serious enough. I like her more than any one else I've met."

"I see." His father looked at his son seriously. "Still thinking about law school and politics?"

"Yes, I guess so."

"Well, that's a serious career. One in the public eye. I mean, America is becoming more used to these sorts of things. Times change. Kennedy's Catholic, yet he got elected. No one would have thought that was possible not too long ago."

"You're telling me that Anna is an Asian and it might

be a drawback for an American politician to have an Asian wife."

"Yes, I guess I'm saying that. But don't get me wrong about it. You know that it doesn't matter with me or your mother. I think she's a lovely girl. All I'm saying is, give it some serious thought. After all, military servicemen in a foreign country . . . it's an old story. You know what I'm saying."

David McWaters knew his father was not a bigot. His father may be a tough, no-nonsense businessman, but he had always believed in a fair shake for everybody. He was only trying to make sure that David had the best opportunity to get where he wanted to go. Just as he had always made sure of it.

"Thanks, Dad. I—I know what you're trying to do. And I appreciate it." He looked out of the window. He thought of Sanders and the ugly face of Le and Chu—no, Chu was dead. He wondered what they were doing now, and he was surprised to find that he was anxious to get back. Good lord, I miss them. "There's a lot I have to think about," he said quietly, his voice trailing away.

Richard McWaters regarded David with a puzzled look for a moment, and then recognized that his son was now a different man. He rediscovered the same lonely sadness he had felt on the day that David had left home for college, and on the day his boy had ridden his first bicycle.

Felix Corman and an American colonel met the four generals in a hotel room near the Saigon airport. The colonel, thick set, with a heavy belly and sloping shoulders, was an Old Asia Hand, first China and Burma, then Vietnam and the Philippines. He knew each of the Vietnamese generals intimately—their capabilities and their weaknesses. One of them would have made a very good sergeant, which in the French Army he once was. Another had five concubines in expensive apartments around the city. Still another was a capable officer and intelligent enough to lead a government. It was all written down in the dossiers he had prepared for the State Department and in the data entered in the CIA's computers.

The generals were uneasy, concerned about American support.

"I am authorized to discuss a coup. We are ready to help you," said the colonel flatly. He watched the chief of staff warily, the blank-faced general who sat in a corner, so far saying nothing. Ba and the big general and the skinny corps commander, they were committed, but the chief of staff was a fence sitter. He's playing both sides, ready to jump where the wind pushes him, thought the colonel.

"We can operate successfully if we have your full cooperation in the planning of this—er, mission," said the chief of staff, breaking the silence.

"I understand your concern, General, but it would appear—be better if all the planning was done by the appropriate Vietnamese authorities—for your own credibility," replied Felix. The United States was not going to be suckered into that one.

The generals were silent for a moment, looking at each other uneasily. If things went wrong they were ruined.

"The body of Colonel Tho has been found. In the Saigon River. We do not know how much of our planning has been exposed."

"There have been rumors for months. The president is not a fool, but how much can he know?"

The generals looked at each other.

"But we have your commitment? Your support for our move?" asked Ba.

"Of course."

The generals stirred. An airplane roared low over the hotel. One or two of them nodded. The chief of staff suddenly smiled.

17

VOSSENACK RETURNED FROM the conference on Guam, and early the following morning he went with General Bachelor to see President Diem. The president's face looked puffy and swollen. He wandered around the room, restless and tired. The demonstrations by the Buddhists had become more severe and frequent. There were rumors of plots and coups. Diem rambled on for an hour, talking of land reform, his plans for education, the traitorous behavior of those who plotted behind his back. Vossenack and Bachelor listened, stony faced. The ambassador remembered a story that had made the rounds of the Saigon embassies: A Vietnamese captain had been appointed a province chief. After a thorough and conscientious inspection, the captain had concluded that the security situation was very serious and he had little authority to make the necessary changes. He had reported his findings to Diem. The president had him reduced to private and sent back to his old unit.

The president puffed nervously on a cigarette. I wonder how many thousands this man and his brother have murdered, imprisoned, and tortured, thought Vossenack. As Diem's voice faltered and became tired, the ambassador began asking questions, pressing for commitments, asking for detail after detail. The meeting droned on. Diem sweated, looking increasingly uneasy. Finally, the two Americans left and returned to the embassy.

Later that afternoon, tanks moved into position along the boulevard leading to the Presidential Palace. The crews huddled behind their vehicles and in doorways waiting for orders. A truck unloaded a platoon of rangers, who hurried along the wide street and set up machine guns to cover the Palace gates. They knew Special Forces soldiers had moved into the building. It added an uncertainty.

The president first knew a coup was underway when there was a scattering of shots outside the palace, and an airplane roared low over the building. A young aide, his hand shaking, stood at a white telephone and handed the handset to the staring, round-faced president. It was an ultimatum, delivered with no conditions. Diem had almost expected it, but it still came as a shock.

He and the mandarin hurried into an air-conditioned cellar. Who? said the mandarin. As we suspected, Ba and Dang. Dang, that bastard. The brother described the general's maternal ancestry in some detail. And also Minh. That was the biggest blow. If the popular Minh was against them they had no hope. They could hear the faint sound of firing. The Special Forces were loyal. Diem had created them—they were even called "Diem's Angels." Without the president, they faced an unknown future. The firing increased. Another telephone call. The young aide in a white uniform, shivering with fright, answered it. He turned to Diem and the mandarin. It was exile. Nothing else could be considered.

There was still hope that some loyal general would rally to the Diem family. All that afternoon, aides kept on the telephone to the generals scattered around the country. Reminders of favors done. Past help in promotions. Assistance to relatives. But the answers were only evasiveness, and gradually the lines went dead. Diem called Ambassador Vossenack, but the American was noncommittal. He could do nothing without instructions from Washington. It was four in the morning there. If Diem and his family—a slight emphasis—were interested in leaving the country, there was a plane waiting at the airport. Diem slowly put down the telephone, stunned, recognition slamming home. His aides stared back at him. The Americans had abandoned him, perhaps had even encouraged the coup.

Diem and his brother realized that time had run out. They looked at each other, the fear heavy in the air, aides already edging from the cellar. There was a way out, a final chance of freedom. A tunnel that led outside the Palace. They could escape after dark, find sanctuary with friends in Cholon.

In the early hours of the following morning, they sat together in a small room at the back of a church. The priest's apartment. Their final refuge. Only a few servants were with them now. It was the end. From the priest's quarters they made their last telephone call. Troops were coming for them. Diem, tears running down his face, raged over the betrayal. Generals who should have been arrested and shot long ago. The mandarin listened silently. He thought of his wife and daughter in the United States. His wife had been the one with the will and the real intelligence. She would have acted, taken the right steps. Now it was over. He walked out into the sanctuary of the church. The priest was kneeling before the altar. He glanced at the mandarin, fear glistening in his eyes. There was dread in the air. The president's brother smiled encouragement, and then knelt beside the priest and stared at the crucifix above the altar. His lips moved in prayer. Outside the church there was the sound of vehicles coming to a stop. Shouts and the rush of feet.

Vossenack stared angrily at Felix Corman. Tieless, he'd had only a few hours sleep and was in his office before dawn. "It was tomorrow. It was to have taken place tomorrow at Ben Thong."

Felix shrugged. "They jumped the gun on us. Still, the results are the same. Neatly done. Not too much bloodshed."

"But goddamn it. Anything could have gone wrong. Diem was supposed to have been arrested outside the city on his way to Ben Long. That was the whole idea. This way, he could have held out in the Palace for days. How would it have looked for us?"

"They got him. Him and his brother. It's over. Minh's in charge now."

There was a knock on the door, and the ambassador's secretary barely had time to say "General Bachelor" before the tall, distinguished general was in the ambassador's office. He looked agitated. There were patches of sweat under the arms of his khaki shirt. Even his trim moustache seemed to droop.

"I've just heard from Ba," he burst out. "You wouldn't believe it. They've killed them. Killed Diem and Nhu."

"What!" The color drained from Vossenack's face.

"Oh, shit." Felix shook his head in disgust.

The three men looked at each other in embarrassed silence for a moment. Vossenack appeared drained, suddenly old and gray. It was finally the CIA man who put into words what each was thinking.

"What's the president going to say?"

Neither of them felt like eating, and the silence was heavy, the sound of a ticking clock unnaturally loud. The servants hurried in and out of the room, whispering.

Vossenack put down his knife and fork with a clatter that vibrated in the silence. He was tired. Cable traffic with Washington and CINCPAC in Honolulu had been intense. He had had little sleep. Vossenack glanced at his wife as she picked at her meal. He had the urge to explain it all to her. To make some sense of the past hours. Tell her it was in the best interests of both the United States and the people of Vietnam. The telephone rang again. There was a murmur as one of the servants answered it. Then came the inevitable discreet knock on the door. It was the Embassy public information officer, tired and nervous.

"Excuse me, Mr. Ambassador. The Situation Room at the embassy. A radio net hook-up with Washington has been set for eleven." Vossenack glanced at his watch. An hour.

"Okay, John. I'll be there."

The State Department man hurried out.

Vossenack and Margaret looked at each other. Margaret also felt worn-out. The day seemed to have left an aching hole inside her.

"That'll be Rusk and McNamara. Maybe Bundy." Vossenack sighed. Something he seldom did.

"You know," he began, then stopped. Margaret waited, staring at her husband. Vossenack started again. "I'm getting—well, I don't particularly like this diplomatic life. I'm a soldier. I was thinking," he looked at her, and for a moment she was frightened by his almost imploring look that seemed to beseech her for understanding, "that perhaps I should really retire. Leave this sort of thing to someone else." He stopped again. "Maybe we should buy a small home somewhere. We've never really had a permanent home. Perhaps San Antonio or Pacific Grove in California, near the Monterey Presidio. You know the place. What do you think about that?"

"Oh, Bob, that would be lovely," said Margaret. There were tears in her eyes. "Oh, Bob," she said again.

Vossenack coughed and carefully folded his napkin.

"Well, it's only a thought, of course. I have to see things through here first. But when everything has been straightened out here. Well, maybe I'll find the right moment," he almost smiled, "and call it quits. That is, if they don't want me out of here sooner." He got up to go back to the embassy, absently shuffling some papers for his briefcase.

"Oh, by the way," said Vossenack, "this dedication at Ben Thong tomorrow. It might be better if we go ahead with it. Maintain a continuity. General Minh won't be able to attend, but there's no reason why we can't be there. Don't wait up for me."

"Bob." She raised her hand almost as if to hold him.

"Yes?" he paused by the door.

"Oh, I just wanted to say . . . take care, dear."

"Sure." He smiled suddenly, the first time he had done so in days, and for a moment she saw the young captain again.

18

LAZAR WAS DRESSING carefully. It was important to look like everyone else. Nothing out of the ordinary that would attract the attention of a bored policeman. He looked at himself in a small hand mirror. White shirt, black trousers, like thousands of other Vietnamese. His height was a problem. He stooped slightly and slipped a pair of dark glasses into his pocket. A loyal supporter of the republic. He almost laughed. Carefully he packed the pistol and the three grenades into his briefcase. Then he stuffed in the other clothing he would need. The case bulged, but it held everything. Lazar sat down and smoked a cigarette. He was ready. Sanders was the loose end. He had failed to kill the American—one of a string of failures that gnawed at him, that made him squirm with exasperation. Well, what he was going to do now would redeem himself; it would make up for everything he had lost. It was too late, Sanders would not find him, the deed would be done and he would be miles away and safe before the American could act.

There was a demonstration down the street, cheers and the noise of firecrackers came faintly through the window. Saigon was celebrating the end of the Diem regime. It had presented a complication, of course. At first he had almost panicked. The weeks of planning wasted. His plans destroyed. Then he had thought hard. He sent his men out on the streets with orders for immediate contact with all sources. They had gone knowing that they usually needed time to set up a contact, to prepare the way carefully for their own safety and the security of the network. Yet they had done it without complaint, realizing that they might be rushed into a mistake, a slip that attracted a Surete agent. Already a member of their cell might be sweating in the basement of a police station.

But the information came in quickly. The sources were not aware of his tenuous position with Central Committee. The ceremony at the hamlet at Ben Thong was proceeding. Tomorrow. He savored the word. The history of Vietnam was going to be changed tomorrow. He zipped the case shut and stood up. The prostitute sat in one corner holding her silent baby. She brushed hair out of her eyes and stared back at him, hunching over the tiny child. Lazar's eyes wandered around the room. The gaudy coverlet over the bed. The pictures taped to the walls. Something was not right; for a moment he felt a stab of anxiety. A look, a feeling that left behind it a question. He paused and looked at her for a moment, thinking of the mission, considering the options. He looked down at the case in his hand, the bulge of the gun. There was a tap at the door. He opened it slightly. A few words whispered by a youth in the hall. Lazar glanced back into the room. How mundane it seemed, how improbable a place for a step that would change history to begin. Then he was gone, carrying with him the staring eyes of the prostitute and her baby, dying in her arms.

19

"I GOT THE call from the National Police about an hour ago. When they mentioned a Eurasian, a mixed blood as they put it, I thought we might be interested." Felix looked around the dingy apartment, at the tiny girl sitting on the bed, huddled with the still baby. A Surete man in civilian clothes was talking to her, snarling questions, but she stared at Felix, an imploring hope. By the door stood a policeman.

Sanders opened the plywood wardrobe. Piles of plastic bags, some dresses, and a man's gray business suit.

"Why did she do it?"

"Medicine for the baby. She thinks we can help it. It looks as though it's dying to me, but we'll take it to the embassy clinic, anyway."

Sanders glanced at her. "Probably an opium addict, too."

Another burst of firecrackers on the street. There was a smell of rotting garbage, cooking, urine, and human sweat. Sanders glanced at the pictures of film stars taped to the wall. It could be anywhere, he thought, give or take. Chicago. Rome.

"Well, he was here, all right. This is where he holed up."

"Too bad she didn't call us before he left. Too scared, I guess. But she gave us some names. We're rounding them up now."

The Surete man whispered something to Felix. The

American nodded. The Vietnamese policeman lifted the girl gently by the arm and led her out of the room.

"Looks like she thinks Lazar was up to something. A big mission. He didn't tell her anything, but she felt he was going somewhere to do something special."

Sanders gazed at the gray suit.

Felix sighed. "We'll question her some more at police headquarters. In the meantime, I'll tell the ambassador." He glanced at his watch. "If I can catch him. He should be leaving for the dedication at Ben Thong about now."

Sanders swung round. "What's this?"

"Sort of a showplace for visiting firemen. The ideal Vietnamese hamlet. Your dollars at work, sort of thing. The hamlet just outside of the city that Margaret Vossenack is working with. Diem was supposed to have been there today for a formal dedication. They're going ahead with it, anyway. Vossenack and his wife are going to be there."

Sanders stared at Felix. He remembered now what Margaret had said about the dedication.

"It's a secure area, Lew. Nothing can happen."

But Sanders was already moving fast out the door.

The security chief walked around the village, inspecting it with satisfaction and pride. The paths had been freshly swept. Banners hung between houses. ("HONOR OUR WONDERFUL COUNTRY," "HURRAY FOR THE ARMY," "WELCOME U.S.A.") Near the center of the village they had built a small platform hung with lanterns and a large banner in English—"WELCOME AMBASSADOR VOSSENACK." Two Army technicians were wiring a microphone to several speakers. A group of small children ran past dressed in their best clothes. The security chief glanced at his wristwatch. Two hours to go. He stopped and called to one of his civil guards to bring water for the drooping plants embedded in the red soil alongside the path. The mayor of the village, the schoolteacher, and two of his aides were standing near the schoolroom, deep in conversation. Rehearsals had been going on for weeks. The school had been freshly painted. The security chief waved to them and walked on, intending to inspect the positions of the guards near the periphery of the hamlet. An immense army truck was parked near the main entrance to the village. What is that doing here? In the corner of his eye the security chief caught a glimpse of a young man, one of the new refugees in the village from some hamlet in the delta he had never heard of, hurry into a house. The young man was dressed in black work clothes. The security chief stopped, annoyed. Everyone was supposed to be in their best clothes today. Had he no respect for today's events? The visit of high dignitaries from the capital? He would bring shame to the village. To the security chief, like all Vietnamese, his village held an immensely important place in his life. The village was more than a home, it was the world. There was a saying in Vietnam that the Emperor's law stops at the village gates.

The security chief walked up to the house. He would tell the young man that he should be grateful he lived in such a fine place. The house was a small one, shared by several youths who had recently moved into the hamlet. The security chief ducked under the low thatched eave and knocked impatiently on the door. The murmur of voices inside abruptly stopped. He pushed open the door, about to call out when he stopped. Inside, his glance took in the men crouched, startled, staring back at him, the man wearing an Army combat uniform, the weapons on the floor. In an instant, the security chief realized all this and much more, and as he opened his mouth to yell, a hand clamped down over it. Arms grabbed him, dragging him down, and he had just time to see the knife and the grim faces above him before the knife plunged down and he died, his hands reaching up in supplication.

"You must be happy about today." Vossenack sat relaxed in the rear of the big limousine, his hand on a strap.

Margaret smiled. "It was a lot of work, but I'm sure it will be worth it. The hamlet looks quite nice now. This is a very proud day for them."

The big limousine coasted along easily, its hydraulic shocks smoothing out the rutted road that led out of the city. Two motorcycle outriders from the National Police, white uniforms sparkling, flanked the front fenders, small stars and stripes fluttering, while behind a long convoy of limousines and sedans carried American and Vietnamese officials. Further back in the procession were several carloads of military police and Surete men.

Vossenack gazed out at the calm countryside, watching the square rice paddies drift past the window. He gestured behind them. "Our friend Sanders is back there. Insisted on coming. McWaters and that Vietnamese sidekick of his, too. Think something might happen today, I guess. You never know with Sanders." He had been told about the raid on the apartment before they left, but he said nothing to Margaret.

His wife stared past the stout chauffeur to the stretch of highway ahead lined wth knots of children and college girls in white *ao dais* and round straw hats. Small flags waved, the stars and stripes and the red bars of the Vietnamese republic. She waved back at them. Robert wondered why she was so quiet. She must be nervous.

"Quite a turnout," said the ambassador. "I didn't realize this meant so much to them. Too bad Big Minh couldn't be here today. I think it would have done a lot for the new government. These things are important."

Margaret smiled. "I'm sure the people in the hamlet

will be proud of whomever comes to the inauguration, dear. They'll be especially proud of having the American ambassador in their village."

Vossenack glanced at his watch. "Well, I hate to say this but I hope it doesn't last very long. Sorry, but I have cables to get out this afternoon and a meeting with Minh scheduled for four."

"It shouldn't take too long, dear," said Margaret, "just a few speeches."

The limousine moved on smoothly. The people on either side were a blur of fluttering flags.

Sanders stared out grimly at the knots of waving people along the road.

"I can't see how anything can happen here." McWaters was affected by the strange silence of the husky man. He tried to sound reassuring, but knew it had no effect. There were three of them crammed in the back seat, a silent Surete policeman sharing the sedan. Le sat in the front seat with the driver. They could see little ahead except the rear of the sedan in front of them packed with people.

"Never underestimate your enemy, Davey."

"Well, we have enough manpower."

Sanders grunted. "We're a long way back. We should be up closer, near the ambassador's car. In fact, we should be in front of it."

National Assembly politicians and embassy officials had the place of honor near the front of the procession. Sanders tried to see around the car ahead of them. The feeling of foreboding hung over them like a pall.

Lazar watched the young man approach through the tables and sit down. He looked nervous, sweating badly.

"It will be over soon, my friend," Lazar smiled at the

young man kindly. "We make history today. You will be honored."

The young man nodded, eyes glistening.

"The explosives are set?"

The young man nodded again, eager for it to start.

It was almost comfortable here, sitting at an outdoor table. A pleasant café. Inside he could hear the owner scolding a careless employee. Lazar relaxed back in his seat, smiling. It was a fine afternoon. Across the rutted asphalted road, peasants worked in the paddy fields, working without cease, ignoring the crowd that was gathering in front of the row of houses and shops. An army truck drove past in a cloud of red dust.

He glanced at his watch. The second hand swept around. In spite of himself his heart began to pound. He could see everything so clearly. It was if he wanted to savor it all, keep the feeling imprinted in his mind forever—the moment when history changed. The distant hills stood out sharp against the pale sky. The taste of the beer was like nectar. An exultation swept through him. The moment had come.

He smiled at the sweating young man in the seat across from him. "It is time, Lanh." The other man got up quickly. His eyes met Lazar's for a moment. Then he walked swiftly back into the café and out the back door. Lazar looked around for a moment, then followed him, strolling. Two old men sat in one corner talking to the proprietor. They never noticed him. Lazar walked through the cramped dirty kitchen. A man was working at a sink and didn't look up. At the back of the café, Lazar pulled a cord in a rain barrel, pulling up a plastic-wrapped package. Two more young men appeared beside him, squatting. Lazar handed one several grenades, another a pistol. He quickly assembled the AK-47, his hands moving over the parts expertly. In the distance, he heard the sound of a labored engine. A huge army truck was grinding along the road. He snapped a magazine into the assault rifle, then covered it with a plastic raincoat. Outside on the roadway a thick crowd had gathered. Children waved flags. The army truck came on, its gears grinding as it picked up speed.

Lazar stood up. He stared for a moment at the schoolchildren waving, standing in groups in front of their teachers. In the distance came the faint sound of cheering and clapping. He smiled and waved his men to their positions.

Margaret waved through the limousine window.

"I think everything is going to be all right," she said.

He misunderstood her, his mind on the past twenty-four hours.

"Yes," he said, absently. "We have no choice but to recognize them now, but I think we did the right thing."

The limousine edged over to the side of the road as a big army truck approached, driving down the center of the road. The young driver seemed to stare ahead as if he didn't see the procession of big limousines, the fluttering flags. The crowd was particularly heavy on this stretch of road, almost a solid line in front of a row of houses and shops; on the other side the open paddy fields. Margaret glimpsed a small outdoor café, part of it a bar with a painted sign, "Texas Bar" and a cactus.

"He's not giving us much room," said Vossenack irritably. The forward outriders had moved in closer to the side of the roadway. "Sound your horn, driver."

The sense that something was wrong came as a sickening shock. She felt almost paralyzed. Her mouth opened to shout a warning, to say something, anything, but no sound came. She stared at the approaching truck, powerless to move.

The truck edged toward them. The ambassador's driver honked in frustration, trying to keep the wheels of the heavy automobile from edging over the soft shoulder of the road and going into the small ditch that surrounded the paddy field. Children waved. Youths, young men and women, seemed to bend forward as if to peer into the ambassador's car. They did not smile.

"Robert," she choked out his name.

What happened next took only seconds.

The chauffeur was still honking as the army truck sideswiped an outrider, sending him smashing into the other motorcyclist. Both careened into the ditch. The huge truck barreled forward, colliding with the ambassador's limousine with a grinding crash, smashing along its side, ripping off chromed trim, the outside rearview mirror disintegrating. A window shattered. The chauffeur sawed frantically at the wheel, but the big auto rolled into the ditch, sending up a shower of muddy water. It shuddered to a halt, tilted almost onto its side.

The truck broke free from the limousine, pieces of broken plastic taillight tinkling on the road, then braked, swerving, coming to rest across the road, blocking off the ambassador's car from the rest of the convoy. A limousine following closely behind the ambassador's car, carrying members of the National Assembly, collided heavily with the side of the truck, its hood sailing into the air. Vietnamese spilled onto the asphalt.

Margaret caught a glimpse of the driver jumping from the truck. He had something in his hand. The rear window of the limousine shattered, glass showered over her. Robert pushed her down to the floor of the car. She heard the sound of rapid firing. The ambassador was gripping the door handle, trying to get out of the limousine, but it had tilted at an angle, the door wedged against the muddy side of the ditch.

No, no, Margaret tried to reach him, to keep him inside the car. Bullet holes appeared in the windshield, more glass cascading over them. For a moment she thought everyone was firing at their car. Children ran wildly, a schoolteacher sprawled in the roadway, blood splashed across her white *ao dais*. The procession of automobiles had piled to a stop. Men were running, several cars smashed together.

Sanders jumped from the sedan, pistol in hand, shouting for McWaters and Le to follow him. A Vietnamese Surete man was kneeling, firing at the crowd. People were scattering. Sanders kicked the Surete man out of the way and ran forward but collided with a mob of panicked politicians and embassy staff. People were running across the road. He couldn't see around the army truck up ahead. The café suddenly erupted with a terrific explosion, chairs and glass showered down on the road. A man spun around, holding a face cut to ribbons.

"Get to the ambassador," yelled Sanders. He was on his knees, trying to stand, blood running from a cut forehead.

Another explosion. A young Vietnamese, his face a mask of contorted hate, threw a grenade toward the packed officials and the running security men, desperately trying to get through them. It exploded in front of Sanders, its blast cutting down two military policemen. Le, trying to help Sanders to his feet, emptied his automatic pistol at the terrorist, bringing him down as he tried to run.

Vossenack, still trying to open the car door, stared back at his wife. She was huddled on the floor of the limousine, tears blurring her mascara across her face. He saw her lips move. She seemed to say Robert again.

With a final shove, he opened the door wide enough to squeeze through. He fell onto his knees in the muddy ditch. The ambassador stood up. Things seemed to be moving in slow motion. He felt amazingly alone amidst all the violence. A memory flashed into his mind of the time, during the war, when he had been on MacArthur's staff, and he had gone forward one day to visit a combat battalion in New Guinea when suddenly the Japanese had attacked. He remembered again the metallic taste of fear, the adrenalin-flowing, gut-wrenching feeling that his life was in the balance. Vossenack stood ankle-deep in the watery mud beside the fields. Smoke from the burning café drifted across the road. His chauffeur was slumped back in his seat with blood running across his face. Another shop exploded. Smoke and flames gushed into the sky and debris rained down around the limousine. Beside the army truck, its driver was lying in a pool of blood, on his face a terrible grin as if death was a comfort. Something suddenly ricocheted off the roof of his limousine. I'm under fire, he thought. Civilians were cowering behind the overturned tables in front of the burning café. Children were running out into the paddy field. Someone was screaming somewhere. He saw a young girl, no more than a child, lying in the road. She was clutching the American flag. No, not the children. Must draw fire from the children. He walked out into the middle of the road. Margaret had pulled herself up and was trying to open her door, but the angle of the automobile made it too heavy for her. He caught a faint glimpse of her as she pounded on the thick smoked window. Her mouth was moving, calling to him, but he heard no sound. "It's all right, dear," he said. He smiled at her, and then something hit him with a terrific blow that knocked him down, sprawling in the road. He tried to get up, brushing futilely at the dirt on his coat. Dimly, the ambassador saw a man in front of him, gun raised.

"You can't—" he began to say. He knew that he would die this way, and the last image in his mind was the Japanese running through the jungle toward his foxhole and the realization that through all those years he had held the fear inside. But now, with the joy of discovery, he realized it was gone.

In cold exultation, as if he were seeing himself perform some sacred act of liberation, Lazar fired, the blood erupting on the chest of the American ambassador, then fired again, making sure his shot hit.

"Jai." The cry made Lazar spin around, catching sight of Sanders pounding toward him, throwing aside people in his way. Lazar fired one last burst toward Sanders from the AK-47, missed, then threw away the rifle and dashed across the road. Sanders fired, seeing the shot splatter against a wall above Lazar's head as the Eurasian ran down an alley between two shops. Behind the row of stores, people cowering in bewilderment, Lazar threw himself on the back seat of a motorcycle, its engine already running, and the young driver threw it into gear and roared off along a dirt path toward a line of trees, scattering a mob of running civilians, knocking an old man down, a loud cry as the man's leg snapped like a twig.

Sanders ran desperately, McWaters and Le behind him. Shouldering people out of the way, he reached the ambassador's limousine and caught a momentary glimpse of Vossenack lying in the road and Margaret running to him. He ran between the two shops, leaping a pile of garbage, in time to see the motorcycle with two riders heading into the trees. He leveled his pistol with both hands and fired twice, knowing the range was too far. People screamed again and scattered. He ran back to the roadway, yelling at a police captain, standing bewildered, staring at the mess. "Call, goddammit. Get more men. Surround the area." Le shouted in Vietnamese at the captain, who finally moved.

Sanders pushed his way through the rapidly gathering crowd around the ambassador. Margaret had his head pillowed on her lap. Tears streaked her face, her hair disheveled. Vossenack's blood was turning her hands red. She looked up helplessly, staring at them. Then she screamed.

"Do something." Her face contorted.

Military police were pushing back the crowd. Men were still running. Women ran screaming to huddle over still shapes on the road. The body of the truck driver was being dragged to the side of the road by policemen, his head banging on the asphalt. Later they would find out it was the schoolteacher at Ben Thong. Another VC, wounded, was being slapped, knocked to the ground. A Surete man was kicking him. A siren vibrated in the still, hot air.

Sanders knelt by Margaret's side. He put his arm across her shoulders.

"Margaret," he said gently. "We'll do all we can. An ambulance is coming."

She seemed not to hear him at first as she still cradled Vossenack's head. Then she suddenly threw her blood-stained hand over her face, misunderstanding his intentions.

"No," she screamed, "no."

Two Vietnamese women, mud on their silk dresses, took her by her arms, helped her to her feet. She attempted to reach down as if to touch her husband again. Vossenack's secretary, Susan Neff, tears streaming down her face, ran up and led her away, Margaret staring dazedly at the blood on her hands and dress.

Sanders looked down at the ambassador. Vossenack's eyes were partly open. He seemed to be staring at Sanders, but there was no look of anger on his face—only one of surprise, as if he didn't realize it could be so easy.

A car slammed to a halt and Felix Corman and several other Americans and Vietnamese in civilian clothes jumped out. Attendants were loading the blanket-covered body of the American ambassador into the waiting ambulance. Police and soldiers were pouring into the area. Felix shouted orders to his hard-faced men. He saw Sanders, still with a pistol in his hand, and walked up to him. Felix stared at the husky man for a moment. Sanders was looking dumbly at the ambulance as it began to move off, lights flashing, police shoving people out of the way. Blood was drying on his face, dull red stains on his shirt and the collar of his suit.

"Get him, Sanders." Felix's face was livid, twisted in rage. "Get him."

20

TEN MILES BEYOND Ben Thong, helicopters circling in the distance, Lazar and the driver ditched the motorcycle and switched to a Lambretta three-wheel carrier that had been hidden in a grove of bamboo. The two men, Lazar driving, headed west then swung north to confuse any pursuit. At nightfall, they stopped at Can Dang, a government outpost not far from the Cambodian border. They spent a few minutes chatting with the two lonely soldiers on duty, telling them a story that they were visting relatives at a village further on. Lazar put some paper money in the shirt pocket of the corporal. With no telephone or radio, the soldiers had heard nothing of the events at Ben Thong and were even unaware that Diem was no longer their president.

Past the government post, they followed a dirt path into the jungle and a few miles further on they came to a tiny hamlet of perhaps a dozen houses. Here, Lazar spent the night in the home of the local VC cadre leader, changing from his civilian clothes back into his black VC pajamas. The two men went on the next day, driving northeast through fields of surgarcane and manioc. Their refuge for the night this time was a single house deep in the jungle occupied by two VC guerrillas, a stopping place for couriers with payroll and rice allotments and NLF supply cadres on their way to the Cambodian border to buy personal goods at local markets. Abandoning the Lambretta, they walked down to a small village on the bank of a narrow river. Perhaps a dozen dugouts were pulled up on the bank, and there was a motorized sampan waiting to take them further north. That night Lazar slept in the jungle on a hammock slung between two trees, covering himself with a nylon sheet to ward off the chilling rain.

The next day the two men came to a small town nestled in a valley in the foothills of the central highlands, not far from the Cambodian border. It was an attractive place, built by Annamite Catholics who had come from Saigon and Hue to trade with the hill people, primitive Mois and Hres. The hill tribes lived in crude huts on stilts and believed in tree spirits and ghosts that haunted the jungle. They planted rows of rice and maize on misty slopes, but constantly at the mercy of the weather and marauding animals, they were always starved for protein and supplemented their diet with bats and snakes and the larvae of beetles and butterflies.

The town was linked to the south by a dirt-and-gravel road that meandered through low hills and jungle. At one end, a large church with two spires served the predominantly Catholic population, about two thousand people, and nearby was a mission with a school, a small hospital and an orphanage. Many of the houses were stone, showing the accumulation of a certain amount of wealth. The town was surrounded by fields—sugarcane, rice, and cotton. Fruit trees grew on cleared slopes, and the jungle was opened into glades by woodcutters where buffalo and horses browsed. In the nearby hills were an abundance of game—fallow deer and wild boar; tigers and panthers, attracted by the herds, lurked in bamboo thickets, hunting at night near drinking pools.

It was the town where Lazar was born, where he went to school at the Catholic mission, and where he lived in the house of his grandfather. He sought it now as sanctuary.

The Americans and the Vietnamese police hunted for Lazar everywhere in Saigon and the surrounding areas. With help from the prostitute, her baby under the care of the American military hospital at Bien Hoa, VC cadres were arrested throughout the city. She had not known many names, but some of those arrested, under questioning, gave the police leads to others. The dragnet spread out further. There were reports of a tall Eurasian sighted in Hue, that Lazar was down in Vinh Long in the marshy delta of the Mekong River, that he was already in Cambodia. Suspected NLF agents were arrested everywhere, interrogated, sweated in steamy back rooms of police stations. But, as they sifted through the reports, followed every lead, checked computer runs with lists of names, the Sûrete and the Americans had to admit that the chances of finding Lazar, when so much of the country was controlled by the Vietcong, were very slim.

The ambassador's body was taken back to the United States aboard a U.S. Air Force airplane accompanied by his widow. An honor guard presented arms. Sanders watched from the airport terminal as Margaret Vossenack was helped aboard the plane by Susan Neff. A State Department aide and a nurse were also traveling with her. She was still in a state of severe shock, unable to cope or even comprehend what was happening to her. Sanders watched the aircraft disappear into the lowering sky above the city.

The regional committee chairman, a smiling emaciated man with stiff, brushed-up hair and eyes like cold black flints, leaned closer to the general.

"The *nguy* have not found him yet?" He used the term of contempt, "puppets," for the South Vietnamese government and its troops.

"They are looking in the wrong places. As usual." The general was chewing on a piece of dried fish. The chunk of monosodium glutamate was supposed to make it more palatable, but it did not seem to help.

They were sitting in a large hut, covered with dyed parachute nylon and foliage, one of dozens scattered around the jungle. For this was NLF headquarters west of the Vam Co River, a rugged and forested region on the Cambodian border, a sanctuary for VC bases not far from the area the Americans would eventually call the "Parrot's Beak."

The chairman was eating a piece of meat. It was monkey. "Lazar has been very brave. His act was that of a patriot. Such courage."

"Precisely." The general, small and hunched at the table, picked at the fish and seemed to look off into the distance as if he saw something puzzling that defied explanation.

The general's sparse hair had turned white in recent months, noted the chairman. He seemed more shriveled than ever. Perhaps the malaria was taking its toll.

"Of course," said the general slowly, "his action has brought a certain amount of—*unfavorable* notice to our cause. The reaction of the world bourgeois community has been predictable, but our brother socialists in the revolution have, I regret to say, been disturbed." The general's voice seemed to fade. "It was not expected . . ."

The regional chairman was immediately alert. A subtle change, a hint of what was being thought in Hanoi.

"I'm afraid the, ah, elimination of the American ambassador may not work to our advantage after all," the general went on, speaking quietly, as if he was somehow working something out in his mind. "It may harden the resolve of the Americans. They are already talking of sending in more troops, appointing a new ambassador. Our socialist brothers in other nations feel we have made a mistake."

The regional chairman stirred unhappily. He had known Lazar for some years.

"Unfortunately," the general's voice droned on, "we do not know what the Tiger plans next. Who knows what he might do? There has already been a compromise of some of our cadres in Saigon. You have heard of the arrests."

"A somewhat headstrong man," murmured the regional chairman. "Perhaps his background . . ."

"Precisely," said the general again.

Sanders walked into Felix's office.

"It's time I left," he said. "I want to go back to the States. There's no longer anything I can do here."

Felix looked grimly at the heavyset man. Sanders seemed to have aged since he first saw him in California. His face more craggy, deeper lines etched between the eyes. A look of pain. He seemed older, did not move as easily. Felix wondered if he was sick.

"You think you've failed. You're quitting."

"It's over, Felix."

"No," said Felix, "it isn't. Lazar is still out there. It isn't finished yet."

"Get McWaters, someone else."

"No. You still have a job to do. We'll find him. Then you can leave." As he watched the stocky major walk out of his office, he thought of a report locked in his safe. A few days ago, a police informer had seen Margaret Vossenack with a burly American, a civilian in a tan suit. He sighed. It was a small town. His thoughts turned again to his problem. Results, that's what everyone wanted. And if they didn't get them they found someone else who could do the job. The order from Langley had been explicit. Schofield and Hoyt wanted Lazar dead. He slumped in his chair in the cool, darkened office, his desk piled with reports and computer printouts. He had to get some results soon.

Anna and McWaters had lunch of *cha gio* at the sidewalk café outside the Continental Hotel, near the National Assembly building with its high-domed, concave entrance. Then they wandered, hand in hand, past the coffeehouses and bars along tree-lined Tu-Do Street. The stately thoroughfare was once called Rue Catinat, and in its cafés one could still hear Frenchmen singing the songs of the *légionnaires*. Some of the cafés and shops, McWaters noticed, had bars over the windows to deflect grenades. They reached the end of Tu-Do Street at the Notre Dame Cathedral on Thong Nhut Boulevard, twin-spired and all red brick and granite. To their left, not far away, they could see the Presidential Palace surrounded by sandbags and gun emplacements.

Anna shivered. "I wonder if my country will ever have peace."

Small yellow and blue taxis buzzed along the street, and they walked past bunches of motorcycles, twenty or thirty packed together, guarded by small boys. They turned away from the Palace, passing the American Embassy, waiting for its new ambassador, until they came to a small park with a temple, the tomb of a military hero. Shards of porcelain and glass decorated its facade, and deeply etched into its walls, war horses that pranced and strode majestically on some ancient battlefield.

A fortune-teller with a long white beard and a round hat sat beside a paper sign, and Anna giggled and urged the lieutenant to sit down. Laughter crinkled the fortune-teller's face, and then he looked at McWaters gravely and consulted a sheath of small square notes on his lap. Ah, he said, and shook his head with wonder. Anna translated, smiling. He would be a great man in his own country.

Inside the temple it was murky and dark, the smoke of incense drifting up from giant urns. Priests read prayers from manuscripts surrounded by offerings of ginger blossoms, grapes, and apricots.

Then they strolled along a gravel path, passing huge stone serpents, and watched an old caretaker patiently raking straight, even furrows into intricate patterns. A vendor sold flavored ices and postcards. "I'm leaving Saigon," said McWaters eventually. "My orders are cut."

Later, in the bedroom of her apartment, he touched her hair gently, as though it was the most tender, precious thing he could ever touch.

"I'm going home," he said. "Come back with me to the States. You'll have a good life. Away from . . . the trouble here. Come with me."

She held him closely as if a part of her was being torn away. He saw she was crying. And he knew that he would always feel, for the rest of his life, a terrible longing. He whispered to her, holding her, stroking her breasts and thighs, and felt her body meld to his, the shadow of the ceiling fan flickering across their bodies, and he moved over her gently, and they became lost together, as though they were in some far-off place, a world of their own.

Sanders's team did not receive a break until a week after the death of Ambassador Vossenack. A Surete detective had a routine meeting in the back room of a Cholon restaurant and bar with one of his contacts, a man who dealt in black-market goods and arranged the sale of weapons to the Vietcong for an ARVN corps commander. The contact was a young round-faced man, already growing fat, who ate surrounded by an array of dishes, one of the bar "hostesses" standing behind him. There was a rumor, he said, wiping rice grains from his chin, about the man who killed the American ambassador. This man, the assassin, grandson of a French officer, was hiding in a place he felt safe. If he would be anywhere, he would be in the town where he was born.

The young man waited until after the detective had left then reached for a telephone. He dialed a number from memory and spoke quietly, telling the woman who answered what he had just told the detective.

"I have heard that the police have recently acquired this information," he added. "It would be wise to act quickly." He put down the telephone and reached out a hand to stroke the thigh of the hostess. The obligations of family and friendship. He sighed. The woman he had called was his distant cousin; they had gone to school together. The cook brought out a dish of *bo bay mon*—beef sautéed in a sauce. Ah! Delicious. He tucked a cloth under his chin.

Sanders looked at Felix, puzzled. "Why would they let us know where he was?"

"He's a rogue elephant. They don't know what he might do next. And if they kill him, what would it do for them? Just another disappearance. But if we kill him, he's another hero dying for the National Liberation Front." Felix paced around the office, stopping to stare out of the window through the plastic Venetian blinds.

He turned to Sanders.

"Did Lazar ever mention to you, when you were in the jungle together, where he was born?"

"I don't know. I remember something about Quang Duc province."

"Think, dammit." Felix shook his head. "Sorry, Lew, I know it's been a long time."

Sanders regarded the CIA station chief with calm composure. "I remember him saying something about a mission school. That's it," he stood up, excitedly. "Le will know, he's from that area."

"Get yourself the equipment you'll need. I'll call MACV. We'll go in with everything we've got."

"No," Sanders stopped Felix. "There's no way we can know how many people he has that are still loyal to him. And we cannot keep an operation like this secret. How much warning does the VC usually get?"

"I don't know—"

"*How long?*"

"Anywhere from eight hours to—" Felix gestured, "days."

"We'll lose him again just like last time. If he doesn't hear that we're on the way, he'll simply disappear into the jungle when he hears our choppers and stay there while we charge around the town looking for him."

Felix waited, knowing what Sanders was going to do.

"I'll get him. Just me, McWaters, and Le. It's the best way."

"McWaters is leaving. In fact, he's leaving the navy. He's only got a few more days to go."

"He'll come with me. If I ask him. We'll get Lazar."

"He may not be there, of course. He may have rejoined his unit—what's left of it. Or gone to NLF headquarters near the border."

"Vietcong come and go," said Sanders. "Jai will lie low for a while until the fuss dies down. He'll sound out the regional committee to see how they feel about him now. It's the best chance we have of getting him."

Felix nodded slowly. "Okay, Lew, go ahead. He always was yours."

The young woman hung up after the call from her cousin and sat on her bed for a moment, thinking desperately. She knew she had little choice. She stubbed out her cigarette and dressed quickly—jeans, a white blouse,

203

sandals, a nylon jacket. She packed a few things in a soft bag, then covered her hair with a bandanna and slipped on a pair of dark glasses. In half an hour she was behind the wheel of her car and leaving the city.

21

THEY LEFT AT night, an army truck taking them the first leg of the journey, forty miles north of Saigon. Then they struck off across the open paddy fields toward the wooded foothills, the taillights of the truck disappearing in the distance and the engine groaning away, leaving only the sound of millions of insects in the humid air.

Carrying heavy packs and weapons, they marched in single file, following Le's directions, avoiding any contact with villages or government outposts. Their green fatigues were soon black with sweat and soaked with water from the tall elephant grass, their boots and pants' legs covered with mud. They stopped and slept for a few hours until it was daylight and then went on. The country grew more rugged, the scrub and bush giving away to denser jungle, light at first then heavier until they had to chop their way through in some places, always keeping within sight of a river on their right. Soon it was almost impossible to see more than fifteen feet ahead of them and sometimes the barbed vines would be so thick they would get hung up on their clothing so that they had to back up to untangle themselves.

Sanders's breath became labored, and he plodded along slowly until he was third in the column, Le leading. McWaters would look around often to make sure he was still there.

The sun hung in the sky like a white ball, barely penetrating the murky gloom but occasionally blazing down through a break in the trees, and when they took a break they lay gasping in the heat, even Le sprawled on the ground.

At night, Sanders and McWaters slept on the wet floor of the jungle, and the navy lieutenant found himself wishing he had brought a sensible nylon hammock like Le. The three men said little to each other, as if conserving their strength. Yet McWaters was not conscious of his own thoughts, rather he focused on nothing, his mind blank, and from Sanders's empty face he knew the major was also doing the same. They just endured, relying on Le to find his way to their objective.

If McWaters stopped to ask himself why he had come on this mission he would probably have not come up with an answer that was logical. He had only a few more days left in Vietnam. His release from the navy waited for him in San Francisco. When he had been called to the telephone at BOQ, Sanders's voice had seemed remote, tired, as if he, too, was wishing it was over.

"I think we can get him, Davey."

"I'm going home."

There was silence for a moment, a heavy sound of breathing, the silence carrying on until McWaters asked if Le was going. Yes, said Sanders, just us. To finish the job.

"Well, I suppose you need me along to get in your way."

A snort. "Be ready to leave tonight." And Sanders hung up, leaving McWaters listening to the dial tone, feeling the fear knot again in his belly.

They climbed higher into the foothills, having to stop more often to let Sanders get his wind back. The stocky man was drenched in sweat, his breathing hard and labored. He seemed to instinctively hold his chest, but took his hand away immediately if he saw McWaters or Le watching. At night, he shivered, and in the morning his lips were blue. Later, McWaters made him swallow some aspirin and tetracycline tablets, looking down at him helplessly. Le stared at them both, saying nothing.

"We can't go on. We've got to get you back. We can radio for a chopper."

"No." Sanders lurched up, his canteen splashing, and grabbed the lieutenant's belt. "No, goddammit. I just need to rest. We're going to see this one through. Nothing is going to stop us."

"Is Lazar that important? Vossenack is dead. Another ambassador is on the way."

"Yes, it's that important. We—" Sanders choked, gasping, water dribbling down his chin, "must show them."

McWaters squatted beside the sick man.

"Is that really the reason? Is it really the VC? Lazar? Or is it Vossenack?"

Sanders stared angrily at the lieutenant with icy eyes, then looked away.

"I saw the way he died. We owe him. Owe him something," he muttered.

McWaters shook his head and stood up. He looked up at the sky and hoisted his pack onto his shoulders. It held a canvas-covered PRC-25 radio powered by batteries.

"We better move some more while it's still light."

They marched on that day and the next, moving away from the river, their world seeming to narrow to a tunnel under the trees, undergrowth to be chopped away, bamboo towering above them. Monkeys chattered in the foliage, and once they heard the coughing roar of a tiger or a leopard. Swarms of flies and mosquitoes hung over their heads, adding to their exhausted misery. They were climbing more now, through more breaks in the trees. Le moved on ahead, scouting, covering their flanks. He seemed inexhaustible. His ugly face streaming with sweat, yet always cheerful, grinning. He still knew little more than a few words of English, yet, with gestures and some remembered French, they communicated.

As they moved higher into the uplands they saw more three-needled pines and thorny, deciduous trees. They were fighting their way through a dense stand of bamboo, reaching almost a hundred feet high, some the thickness of a man's waist, when Le, who had gone on ahead, came running back. This time he did not smile.

He said something in Vietnamese, then "Town . . . *le ville* . . . it near." He gestured.

McWaters and Sanders stopped, breathing heavily, and looked at each other. They walked on cautiously, avoiding dead branches and twigs. They passed some fields of maize and a few shriveled stands of cotton. The faint sounds of water buffalo snorting came on the wind, and they edged away, not wanting to meet a herdsman or a farmer.

By late afternoon they had maneuvered their way to a low hill above the town where they hid in the dense underbrush. Through binoculars they watched the single street. They saw several dozen Vietnamese. People shopped at a tiny store, old women wandered in and out of the church. A file of children followed a nun across the street. Most of the houses were clustered together, but a few straggled off into the nearby gullies between the hills. On the outskirts of the town were woodsmen's shacks and barns for the animals. Beyond, a river that disappeared into the hills. They watched silently as the sun descended toward the distant mountains of Cambodia, an undulating green across the horizon.

"See anyone that looks like Charlie?" McWaters was eating a packaged food ration.

"No," grunted the major, peering through the glasses. "Looks as though the war has missed this place." He looked at Le. "I don't think we're going to catch sight of him from up here. Le has to go down there and look around."

They explained patiently to the Vietnamese what they wanted. After a great deal of gesturing and repeated "reconnoiter"—which left Le staring in puzzlement—and "camouflage," they were finally able to make the Vietnamese understand. He took some old black pajamas out of his pack and put them on. Sanders suspected that the Vietnamese turncoat carried them with him so that he could desert if it was necessary. Then, taking his machete, Le cut a large pile of dried wood, which he tied into a bundle with a cord. Le grinned at Sanders and McWaters for a moment, his ugly face lopsided. He hoisted the bundle higher and then set off down the hill toward the village. He looked like any other Vietnamese peasant, an itinerant woodcutter. As McWaters watched him go, he realized how much they relied on him, and how uncomplaining the Vietnamese was, and he wondered why Le stayed with them—there must have been numerous opportunities for him to desert. Perhaps Le was like them more than they realized. Perhaps the motivations of people were not so different after all.

As the day turned to evening, they watched the changing shades of green on the distant hills, and mist filled the lower valleys. Night, and Le had still not returned. Sanders and McWaters huddled beneath their blankets in the damp chill, not daring to light a fire. A gibbous moon shone down on the little town, but there was no movement, the only sign of life a shrouded gleam of light in a few windows. A large animal roared in the distance, the sound carried faintly on the wind. They took turns sleeping, the other man occasionally sweeping the town with binoculars, but seeing nothing unusual.

At dawn they each ate a protein bar. The supplies were giving out. In the gray light, they spread out their blankets to dry, crawling around on their hands and knees so as not to give away their position. Sanders shook his head, looking at his soaked boots.

"They've got to come up with better boots than these. I can hardly feel my feet anymore."

They watched farmers ride out of town on bicycles for a day's work in the fields. Children assembled at the mission school, the church bell rang for a few minutes—a distant, dull clang—and a few old men and women appeared on the street.

"Not many young men or women," said Sanders, looking through his binoculars. "Not many teenagers, either."

"Probably in the ARVN," said McWaters.

"Or out there with Charlie."

"Wait a minute. There's someone." Sanders watched as a young man in dark peasant dress appeared and walked toward a large stone house at the end of a street, slightly apart from the others. The major watched him through the glass. There was something different about him—a look, the way he walked. The young man looked around before he went inside the house.

"Peaceful, ain't it?" said Sanders, and then a sound of movement in the brush to their left made them grab for their weapons, rolling away, as Le emerged from the bushes. He no longer had his bundle and his clothes were soaked from the wet vegetation. He gestured toward the town, pointing out the same large house that the young man had entered. It was at the end of the street away from the church.

"La-zar. La-zar. He there."

"How many men does he have—er, *combien de*, damn, ah, *les hommes ya-t-il dans le maison?* OK? Understand?" Sanders pointed, gave the impression of shooting.

Le held up two fingers. "*Et deux femme.*" He gave an impression of an old woman and then of a young woman.

"La-zar, he's there now? *Maintenant*?"

Le shrugged.

"Well, two men, two women—probably servants or relatives," said Sanders to McWaters. "But is he there now? That's the question." Sanders stared at the house through the glasses, then looked at his watch. "Okay, we can't wait, we'll go in now. I don't want any Vietnamese hurt unnecessarily, but we get Lazar."

The question hung in the air. Finally, McWaters said quietly, "Do we kill him?"

Sanders was laying out several grenades on his blanket. He paused for an instant, as if considering. "Not unless we have to. We'll try to bring him out alive." His voice rumbled, and he coughed hard suddenly, almost gagging. He spat into the bushes, and McWaters could tell he was in pain. "No grenades. We're not going to blow up the town."

They checked their weapons and studied the approaches to the house. Their packs and the radio were pushed under some bushes and covered with brush. Le changed back into his uniform and ate a handful of rice. A thin drizzle of rain began. The street in the town looked deserted.

Sanders looked at his watch, his face cavernous. He stifled a cough, then nodded, stood up, and they followed him through the scrub toward the town.

The three of them spread out and walked down through the trees in the somber light, crossing a field toward the houses. A farmer, digging an irrigation trench, stopped and stared at them, perfectly still. Under his conical straw hat, his brown face was fixed, impassive. They passed him and walked on, a dog suddenly barking. McWaters glanced around and saw the farmer hurrying across the field toward some men working in the distance.

"Let him go," muttered Sanders.

They were moving fast now, almost running. The three men leaped a ditch and ran across the road, sending a flock of ducks squawking away.

Sanders gestured, and Le ran for the rear of the house, smashing his way through a gate in a bamboo fence. Chickens fluttered and squawked. A woman's voice called something. McWaters nodded at Sanders and they both ran toward the door. They almost reached it when it opened and a young man stood there. He had a gun in his hand. For a moment, everyone froze and then the Vietcong yelled something and Sanders swung the butt of his carbine like a club, knocking the Vietnamese back into the house, his face bloody. Sanders and McWaters were inside the door in an instant, sweeping the room with their carbines.

Inside, it was cool and dark. Wood beams supported the ceiling. McWaters took in heavily carved, dark brown furniture and expensive rugs in shades of blue and green.

The young man lay on his back in the light from the doorway, moaning softly. McWaters picked up the dropped automatic pistol and stuffed it in his belt then grabbed the Vietnamese by the shirt collar and dragged him into the house. More dogs were barking outside.

A stairway went up into darkness at the end of a hall. Silently, Sanders edged toward it.

Somewhere there was a sound, a footstep.

McWaters, watching the man lying on the floor, moved further into the house. On a heavy bureau, he noticed an old photograph in a frame: a man and a woman in traditional Vietnamese dress with a young boy between them. The man looked almost European, the woman tiny beside him.

A noise from the back of the house, glass breaking. Sanders moved slowly down the hallway, his gun sweeping a room to the right. He looked up at the ceiling, trying to stifle a grimace of pain, his breathing heavy.

"Jai," he suddenly called, his voice hoarse. "It's Lewis."

There was no sound from the house.

"Jai. Give yourself up. It's over." Sanders edged toward the stairway.

McWaters moved further into the house, still glancing back at the Vietnamese, who lay moaning on the floor. His nerves were like thin wires, a pounding in his chest.

Sanders motioned him to stop. Then the major slowly began to ascend the staircase, placing each foot carefully before shifting his weight.

A door creaked.

At the top of the stairs was a landing with a low wooden rail. As Sanders's head came level with it he saw a long hallway and doors leading to the bedrooms. He moved swiftly, stepping across the hallway, his back to the wall. At the bottom of the stairs McWaters watched him. He saw Sanders move slowly down the hall. The major pushed open the door of one room, glanced inside, then moved on carefully.

There was a movement behind McWaters, he swung wildly.

It was Le.

McWaters motioned him to watch the young VC, then followed Sanders up the stairs. He saw the burly man try the door of a room, then thrust it open and disappear inside.

A high pitched woman's scream echoed through the house. Then silence.

Sanders reappeared dragging an old Vietnamese woman by the arm. "Calm down, calm down," he was saying. The woman was crying, shaking in terror. "Take her downstairs," he said to the lieutenant. He swiftly searched the last upstairs rooms then came down to where they were all gathered.

Le had managed to calm the terrified woman. She was sitting on a chair, gray hair falling over her eyes, but still trembling at the sight of the armed foreigners.

While Le watched both the Vietnamese, Sanders and McWaters searched the rest of the house and the two outbuildings, but of Lazar, there was no sign.

The assassin was not there.

22

THE INFORMATION WAS not long in coming. One look at Le's wicked, ugly grin and the bayonet knife he pulled from his belt, and the young Vietnamese, no more than seventeen years old, began to talk, his words pouring out in a torrent. The translation was slow, Le mixing Vietnamese, French, and English, but eventually it became clear. Lazar and a young woman had left the day before. Where? The young man hesitated, looking at the old woman. She started at him vehemently, cackling something until Le shouted at her, apparently the Vietnamese equivalent of shut up because she subsided into angry silence.

"*Xa Loi*," said the young man. A Buddhist temple, further into the mountains, at the head of the valley, perhaps on this side of the border, perhaps in Cambodia, no one knew for sure.

The old woman muttered something, and the young man hung his head, not looking at her. An ugly bruise was appearing across half his face, and one eye was closing.

"Ask him how far."

He wasn't sure, perhaps sixteen kilometers, maybe more. You followed a track that led from the village. The monks would occasionally come down to barter vegetables for chickens and pigs, but not often; the Catholics in the town did not like them.

"Why is he still here? Why isn't he up at the temple with Lazar?"

The young man hung his head. Le prodded him. He came back to get batteries for the radio. They had forgotten them. From the way he said it there was no doubt that the fault was his.

"Ask him who the young woman is."

But here Le drew a blank. The young man said he didn't know, but he thought she was a woman from the city.

"We going up after him?" said McWaters.

"We didn't come this far to go away empty-handed."

McWaters and Le brought down the packs and the radio, and they got ready to move on. The young VC was roped to Le. In the kitchen they found some cooked rice and *cha gio,* fried rolls filled with pork and vegetables. They wrapped a dozen in paper and stuffed them in a backpack. As they walked out of the house, cramming handfuls of rice into their mouths, the old woman exploded into a torrent of curses, shaking her finger at the young Vietnamese, who seemed glad to leave.

A small crowd of people had gathered outside the house, but they stayed back as the armed Americans and their prisoner walked out. Sanders waved them back, and they parted, letting them through, staring at the strange sight of foreigners in uniform, sweaty and big.

They walked part of the way up through the town, the townspeople avoiding them, and then swung onto a hard-packed track that led upward through the trees toward the Cambodian border, following the river. McWaters saw a Vietnamese Catholic priest staring at them from the steps of the church, but he made no move to approach.

"Lazar knew we were coming, Lew."

Sanders nodded, grimly, saying nothing.

The track climbed through stunted trees, heavy brush, and tall stands of elephant grass and, occasionally, past huge teak trees with immense crowns of foliage. Ahead, they could see mountains that reached to more than three thousand feet. From a width of a mile or so the valley quickly narrowed until the track wound upward between angular hills, the grade gradually becoming steeper.

The river swirled, stronger, and bent back on itself, cutting between steep embankments. Here and there, it roiled over snags of tree branches and bamboo brought down from higher up in the hills. Mosquitoes buzzed around them in annoying clouds, and they had to stop and rub on repellant. It was still overcast and a thin drizzle continued to fall, and they could at least be thankful that it was not hot.

Sanders was finding the climb so difficult they had to stop every fifteen minutes for him to rest. He looked exhausted, his breath labored and sweat coursing down his heavy features, hair plastered to his forehead.

"Lewis, give it up," said McWaters. "What are you trying to prove?"

"No, goddammit," snarled Sanders. "That bastard's not going to kill an American ambassador and get away with it." He lay back against the steep side of the trail, breath rasping.

"I can come back with a ranger company, a team of Special Forces."

"No, do you think Lazar is stupid? We don't know when Junior over there was due to report back. If he doesn't show, Lazar will hop over into Cambodia or head north. We'll never get him."

McWaters looked down at the heavily built man with exasperation. "What is it, Lew, Margaret Vossenack?"

Sanders stared up at the young lieutenant in icy rage, and then the anger faded.

"How did you know about that?"

"She came out to the camp looking for you. I just guessed that—well, you know."

"Well, let me tell you, Lieutenant McWaters, nothing came of it. It's over. Finished. D'you hear? And Margaret Vossenack is a lady. You'll forget about it."

"Right, Lew. I understand," said McWaters gently.

They pushed on, climbing higher, Le dragging along the VC prisoner, once cuffing him when the youth didn't move fast enough. They had been marching for about five hours, when they saw the temple ahead.

It was built on a knoll above a bend in the river, which ran through steep hills, almost a gorge, backed by a stand of dense bamboo and heavy brush. But beyond this was an open, flat meadow with a few cattle and further up, some fields. Low mountains, covered with greenery, rambled off into the distance. The building was not large, about two stories high with light-colored walls and a swaybacked roof covered with greenish brown tile. A small tiered pagoda jutted up at one end. The temple was enclosed with a low wall, and to one side were some outbuildings that looked as though they held livestock.

They scrambled off the trail into the underbrush, and Sanders searched the building through his glasses.

"Can't see anybody. Probably all inside or up there in the fields." He lowered the binoculars and stared up at the temple reflectively.

"We can't just go barging in there shooting. It's a religious place," said the lieutenant.

"I know." Sanders glanced up at the sky. "But we can't wait."

They ate a hurried meal of the Vietnamese food and the last of their protein bars, sharing it with the VC.

"Le, tell him if he so much as farts we'll cut his heart out," said Sanders.

Le's rapid Vietnamese and appropriate gestures

seemed to do the trick. The youth cowered, hugging himself miserably.

Sanders tried to stand up, but his legs seemed to give way and he sat down heavily.

"Shit," he growled.

McWaters had to help him to his feet.

They walked up to the temple in a line, Sanders leading, Le and the prisoner bringing up the rear.

As they followed the path up toward the temple, it broadened, and as they got nearer to the building, it was marked with cut logs. Two Buddhist monks in saffron robes came out of one of the outbuildings carrying buckets of water. They stopped and stared when they saw the Americans. There was a wicker gate in the stone wall surrounding the temple, and they pushed it open and walked along a gravel path up to heavy, ornate double doors recessed into an overhanging entry.

There was a peculiar smell in the air, a strange mixture of incense and manure and a musty odor of wet clay.

The two monks continued to watch them without moving. A young monk, no more than a boy, appeared at the side of the building carrying a broom. He, too, stopped and looked.

"What do we do now?" said McWaters. There was no sound from within the building.

"I guess we knock."

Sanders rapped at the door.

There was the sound of shuffling feet, and an elderly monk opened the door, staring at them, blinking as if the light hurt his eyes.

"Tell him we would like to speak to the head man, the abbot or whatever he's called."

The monk listened to Le and then closed the door. They could hear his footsteps receding. The two Americans glanced at each other. The three monks watching them had still not moved. After what seemed like many minutes, the door opened again, and the monk motioned them inside. When they started to walk in, he put his hand up in protest and said something in Vietnamese.

"He say . . . guns, *ici*," said Le.

Reluctantly, they left their weapons and packs at the door and followed the monk down a musty-smelling hall lined with carvings of the Buddha set into shallow niches. The monk motioned them into a small room with whitewashed walls. Another elderly monk, almost identical in appearance to the first, sat behind a low table. On it was a stack of old manuscripts, roughly bound between boards, and a bowl filled with the blossoms of some flower. The elderly monk, evidently the abbot, motioned them to sit down on a strip of rush matting. The room felt cold and damp.

"Le, tell the abbot that we represent the—" began Sanders, but the abbot interrupted.

"*Parlez-vous le francais?*" he said.

"Your French is better than mine, Davey," said Sanders. "Go ahead. Tell him we represent the governments of South Vietnam and the United States. We are here to apprehend a criminal, a terrorist, who has murdered the United States ambassador. We believe this man, Lazar, is now here in this temple."

The lieutenant explained this to the abbot in French, and when he had finished there was a moment of silence.

"Who is this man?" said the abbot, gesturing at the VC prisoner, still bound to Le.

"This man is a terrorist, a companion of the criminal we seek. He is now our prisoner, and we intend to take him back with us and hand him over to the government," said McWaters.

The abbot seemed to think, his face expressionless.

"What will happen to this man, Lazar, who you call a terrorist?"

"We will take him back with us to stand trial for murder."

"Lazar thinks of himself as a patriot. A man trying to drive out the invaders of his country."

"The murder of an ambassador cannot aid his cause. It is an act that revolts the civilized nations of the world. It has been condemned by all nations—even those sympathetic to the aims of the National Libreration Front. If the murderer is not apprehended, it can only bring disgrace upon your country."

The abbot stared at McWaters, then said something to the VC prisoner in Vietnamese, a sharp question. The young man mumbled something in reply, hanging his head. It seemed to confirm something. The abbot nodded.

Le leaned forward. "Charlie say La-zar, ah, cause die American Voss'nack," he said quietly.

There was quiet for a moment in the small room.

Somewhere a deep gong vibrated for a moment.

The abbot got to his feet, amazingly lightly for so old a man. They all stood up.

"*Venez avec moi*," said the abbot. He led them down another hall, past closed doors, the sound of a chant, to another door, which let them out into a small yard at the side of the temple. The drizzle had stopped.

The abbot pointed, speaking in French. "Follow the path. It will take you to a small house. About one hundred meters. Lazar is there." He turned quickly and went back into the temple, closing the door firmly.

They collected their weapons and packs, and then followed the winding path through a grove of bamboo and pine until they saw the roof of a small house ahead. Smoke drifted from a chimney.

"Okay, we move fast," said Sanders. "Leave the packs and the radio here. Le, you'll cover the back and keep the prisoner with you. If he does anything, anything at all, kill him." He stared grimly at the young VC to make his meaning clear. "Davey, we'll go in through the door. You'll cover me."

They moved forward swiftly, Le and the VC branching off toward the rear of the building, Sanders and McWaters running for the small front door. As they got closer, McWaters could see it was no more than a small, clay-dabbed cottage, probably with two or three rooms. A retreat within a retreat. They ran through a small vegetable garden, neglected and overgrown. He barely had time to take in everything before Sanders had kicked hard at the small door, bursting it inward, and then they were inside, covering the two people in the room with their guns. Sitting at a small table, looking stunned and disbelieving, were Lazar and Anna Vo.

"Don't move," rapped Sanders. He was breathing heavily. "Jai, don't do anything foolish. It's over."

Lazar kept his hands on the table. A small tea cup had overturned, and in the silence they heard the drip of the liquid onto the floor.

McWaters was staring at Anna Vo, hurt and confused, not believing that she could be here with an assassin.

"Davey," said Anna. "I thought you had left Vietnam."

"No, not yet," he said. "But perhaps I should have." He stared hard at her. "I'm—sorry to see that you're—one of them. You really fooled me."

"You don't understand, Davey—" Anna started to say, but Lazar spoke for the first time.

"Yen is my daughter," he said.

Both Sanders and McWaters stared at them, stunned.

"But the name—" said McWaters.

"Names are often changed in Vietnam, Davey," said the woman. "Vo was my mother's name, and I'm an actress. It was better if I did not have a French name."

"I'm sorry you're involved with this, Miss Vo or Miss Lazar, whatever your name is, but your father is a wanted man. We have to take him back. Get up both of you and come with us." Sanders gestured, his carbine still pointing at Lazar.

They stood up.

"Lew," Lazar looked anguished, imploring, "my daughter was never in the National Liberation Front. She is not a Communist. She just came up here to warn me because she is my daughter. Let her go. Please. As you used to say, for old time's sake."

Sanders hesitated. He stared tiredly at the young woman.

And then Lazar moved.

He must have had the pistol cocked and ready to fire because in one moment he had pulled the gun from under a cushion on a chair.

McWaters, blocked by Anna, yelled a warning, but Sanders, exhausted, his arms shaking with the effort of holding the carbine, was much too slow. Lazar fired, the noise deafening in the small room.

Anna shrieked.

McWaters saw Sanders thrown back, and as Anna dropped to the ground he fired at Lazar. The assassin yelled something, crashing back against the table, his gun came up, and McWaters fired twice more, sending Lazar smashing to the ground.

McWaters panted, as if he had run five miles. Anna huddled beside her father, sobbing.

The lieutenant moved forward slowly, covering Lazar, his ears ringing. Le and the young VC ran up and stopped in the doorway. The lieutenant looked down at Lazar. The front of the assassin's shirt was soaked in blood, but he was still alive, barely. Anna was sitting beside him, talking to him urgently in Vietnamese, tears running down her face.

Sanders lay crumpled against a wall. For a moment McWaters thought he was dead. Then he saw the husky man was still breathing. Sanders opened his eyes and looked up at McWaters and tried to say something, choked, his legs moving as if he was trying to stand. The bullet had hit him low in the chest and seemed to have ricocheted off a rib, tearing open his side.

Le brought their packs to the door, and they put a dressing on the major's wound. Anna continued to sit by her father, moaning softly.

"Untie him," said McWaters to Le, gesturing at the young VC. It seemed pointless to hold him now. The young man sank down on a chair, staring at the dying Lazar.

McWaters and Le lifted Sanders up to carry him outside, his arms around their necks.

"Wait," he gasped. He looked down at Lazar. The assassin's eyes opened. He stared up at Sanders. Blood oozed from the corner of his mouth. Sanders reached into his pocket, grimacing with pain. A photograph dropped onto the floor beside Lazar. Recognition flooded the assassin's face. His hand moved to touch it. He almost smiled for a moment. Then he shuddered and was still, his eyes open, fixed on the faded image.

They carried Sanders to the small meadow behind the temple and covered him with the nylon hammock, and then they rigged up a tall antenna for the radio.

Sanders face was ashen. His eyes closed. McWaters squatted beside him.

"We reached the Advisory Group at Ban Me Thuot. A chopper's on the way."

The major's eyes opened. He nodded, grimacing.

"What about Anna, Lew?" said the lieutenant.

Sanders's voice rasped, and McWaters had to bend forward to hear him. "Your decision."

McWaters walked back to the house. Anna was still

sitting on the floor by her father. The young man sat in the chair his head in his arms.

"Anna," said McWaters gently, "you're free to go. I'm sorry. So . . . sorry." He stopped. There didn't seem to be anything more he could say.

The woman looked up at him. Her eyes were filled with tears, but she was no longer crying.

"I know, Davey. Somehow," she looked down at her father, "I knew it would happen. But," her eyes on him again, more tears welling, "there was no way I could stop it."

He tried to say something else, but she held up her hand.

"It's all right, Davey. I understand. Please leave me here with him. Lanh will help me bury him. Please go."

He walked out of the tiny cottage, his last view of her still huddled on the floor, her eyes following him, filled with infinite grief.

When McWaters got back to Sanders and Le, the major opened his eyes.

"I've let her go, Lew."

Sanders nodded. "Knew you would. What's going to happen . . . to you and her?" His voice grated.

"No chance. Not now. Perhaps one day I'll come back to Vietnam and see her again. There's always—always another chance for the future."

"I'm sorry, Davey." His breath caught with pain. "Still leaving the navy?"

"Yes. It's time I went on with my life."

"Politics?"

McWaters thought for a moment. "Yes," he said. "But I think I'll be a different kind of politician than I would have been if I had never come to Vietnam. I see things differently now. I hope I know more. At least more about means and goals and how they should be matched, and the differences—and the sameness—in people. I know that many things are relative. But we don't ever compromise with our integrity—not with our honor."

Le was speaking on the radio. The sun was beginning its descent over the Cambodian hills. Sanders coughed hard, and a pink froth formed on his lips. He seemed to be shivering slightly. But he gazed up at the sky with a sense of wonderment, as if a time of trial was over.

The lieutenant looked at Le squatting, smoking a cigarette, looking off toward the mountains to the north. There was something timeless and patient about the Vietnamese man's face, a nobility that had survived for a thousand years. McWaters knew Le would go on surviving, go on living, wherever the world took him.

He patted Sanders's hand.

"What about you, Lew?"

Sanders smiled slightly, his face seemed to be etched with pain, but his eyes were clear. "I've got something to do. You can't become involved with someone's life without taking some responsibility for what happens. You must be answerable for the consequences. I hurt someone, badly,"—a memory of Margaret's pale gentle face as she explained to him her concern for the village—"but perhaps I can make it up somehow. I have a daughter who needs my help and an ex-wife who I let down. I think I'd better start there."

Le suddenly called, his ugly face grinning, pointing off into the distance. McWaters stood up and lit a red flare. The clouds were clearing, it was the last of the monsoon. The two helicopters seemed like distant specks in the sky, coming toward them over the hills, but he knew it was the first step on their road home.

"A FASCINATING PORTRAIT OF TWELVE MEN WHO DREAMED OF SERVING AND LEADING OUR NATION." —Mario Puzo

DUTY, HONOR, VIETNAM
Twelve Men of West Point Tell Their Stories

by Ivan Prashker
0-446-36867-3/$4.95 ($5.95 in Canada)

They are graduates of West Point, drilled in the principles of duty, honor, country; persuaded that there is no substitute for victory. In the compelling tradition of *Nam*, *Everything We Had*, and *Once a Warrior King*, this is a stunning firsthand look at the Vietnam combat experience from the singular perspective of the military officer.

**Warner Books P.O. Box 690
New York, NY 10019**

Please send me ___copy(ies) of the book. I enclose a check or money order (not cash), plus 95¢ per order and 95¢ per copy to cover postage and handling.* (Allow 4-6 weeks for delivery.)

___Please send me your free mail order catalog. (If ordering only the catalog, include a large self-addressed, stamped envelope.)

Name _____

Address _____

City _____ State _____ Zip _____

*New York and California residents add applicable sales tax.

"TAKE(S) THE READER STRAIGHT INTO THE TRENCHES AND FOXHOLES."
—*New York Times Book Review*

In the powerful and best-selling tradition of *Nam*, here is Eric Hammel's highly-acclaimed, two-volume oral history of one of the longest and bloodiest battles of the Vietnam War: Khe Sanh.

☐ **THE ASSAULT ON KHE SANH:**
An Oral History
0-446-36022-8/$4.95 ($5.95 in Canada)

☐ **THE SIEGE OF KHE SANH:**
An Oral History
0-446-36023-6/$4.95 ($5.95 in Canada)

**Warner Books P.O. Box 690
New York, NY 10019**

Please send me the books I have checked. I enclose a check or money order (not cash), plus 95¢ per order and 95¢ per copy to cover postage and handling.* (Allow 4-6 weeks for delivery.)

___Please send me your free mail order catalog. (If ordering only the catalog, include a large self-addressed, stamped envelope.)

Name _____

Address _____

City _____ State _____ Zip _____

*New York and California residents add applicable sales tax.

WARNER TAKES YOU TO THE FRONT LINES.

- □ **SOME SURVIVED** by Manny Lawton
  (H34-934, $3.95, USA) (H34-935, $4.95, Canada)
  A World War II veteran and prisoner of war recounts the true story of the Bataan Death March—a harrowing journey through dust, agony and death at the hands of the Japanese.

- □ **BIRD** by S. L. A. Marshall
  (H35-314, $3.95, USA) (H35-315, $4.95, Canada)
  The brilliant account of the First Air Cavalry's heroic defense of the strategic Vietnam landing zone called "Bird."

- □ **FOX TWO** by Randy Cunningham with Jeff Ethell
  (H35-458, $3.95, USA) (H35-459, $4.95, Canada)
  A fighter pilot's birds-eye view of air combat in Vietnam, written by a decorated Navy jet commander.

**Warner Books P.O. Box 690
New York, NY 10019**

Please send me the books I have checked. I enclose a check or money order (not cash), plus 95¢ per order and 95¢ per copy to cover postage and handling.* (Allow 4-6 weeks for delivery.)

___Please send me your free mail order catalog. (If ordering only the catalog, include a large self-addressed, stamped envelope.)

Name _____

Address _____

City _____ State _____ Zip _____

*New York and California residents add applicable sales tax.